LB.

F
MAC

Riches to Rags Bride

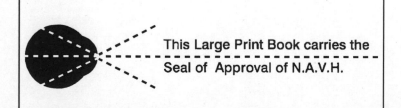

This Large Print Book carries the
Seal of Approval of N.A.V.H.

RICHES TO RAGS BRIDE

MYRNA MACKENZIE

THORNDIKE PRESS
A part of Gale, Cengage Learning

Detroit • New York • San Francisco • New Haven, Conn • Waterville, Maine • London

GALE
CENGAGE Learning®

LIBRARY OF CONGRESS CATALOGING-IN-PUBLICATION DATA

Mackenzie, Myrna.
    Riches to rags bride / by Myrna Mackenzie. — Large print ed.
      p. cm. — (Thorndike Press large print gentle romance)
    ISBN-13: 978-1-4104-4279-6(hardcover)
    ISBN-10: 1-4104-4279-9(hardcover)
    1. Women's shelters—Fiction. 2. Chicago (Ill.)—Fiction. 3. Brides—
Fiction. 4. Large type books. I. Title.
PS3613.A2727R53 2011
813'.6—dc23   2011035388

Published in 2012 by arrangement with Harlequin Books S.A.

Dear Reader,

I've always been fascinated by Cinderella stories — tales of strong women who finally catch a break and fight through to their happily-ever-afters — but what about the opposite, the woman who appears to have everything and then loses it all? It's not a question I, as a writer, ask myself all that often.

But then Genevieve Patchett slipped into my thoughts. Born to wealth, she's always had plenty of pretty, totally impractical clothes and a closet full of shoes. Throughout her life, she's been able to buy pretty much anything she wants. And to top it off, she's the daughter of very famous parents.

In short, she seemed to have it all. Until she didn't. Because one day, when she put her trust in the wrong person, it all vanished. Just like that. No money, no home, no place to go, no one to turn to, nothing left but utter terror. And that was when she caught my attention and refused to let go. Because who, after all, can help but worry about someone so ill prepared to face a dark and dangerous world?

I couldn't, but I wasn't so sure about the hero, Lucas McDowell. Lucas has been deserted and forced to fight to make his way alone. Always. He swears he doesn't have a heart and doesn't want one. And he's learned not to trust. Anyone. Especially not pampered rich girls.

Oh, yeah, Lucas's attitude was a concern. And Genevieve, it appeared, wasn't going to make it easy on him. I didn't really know what would happen if they spent too much time together. Disaster was a real possibility.

But I had to find out. I hope you enjoy their rocky backward Cinderella story.

Best wishes,
Myrna Mackenzie

CHAPTER ONE

Genevieve Patchett stared at the solid mahogany door of the office where she was scheduled to have the first job interview of her life. Despite being twenty-six, she had an empty resume, a lot of explaining to do and a stack of bills so high that her throat closed up every time she looked at it. And Lucas McDowell, the man who held her future and her very survival in his hands, was reputed to be a cold, hard businessman who only hired the best. She was *not* the best.

Reaching for the doorknob, her hand trembled and she gripped the knob tightly, turning her attention to getting in and trying to at least appear competent. She had to have this job. Her friend Teresa had gone out on a limb to get her this interview.

Genevieve opened the door just a touch . . . and immediately stopped. Muffled, angry sounds came from the other side of the door. Female sounds.

Getting louder.

Suddenly the door flew open, and she found herself staring at a tall, frowning brunette beauty.

Gen took a step back, and the woman barked out a harsh, ugly laugh. "Oh, don't run away, sweetheart. He's all yours now. Just be careful and don't fall for him. He doesn't have a soul." Tossing her head, the woman glanced back over her shoulder. "Lucas, your next victim is here."

With that, the woman moved down the hall, and Genevieve could finally get a good look at the broad-shouldered, dark-haired man standing behind a desk. For half a second she wondered if running was an option. Lucas McDowell might be wearing a suit most men couldn't afford to even dream of owning, but he had the strong-boned face of a street fighter, gunmetal-gray eyes that seemed to see right through to all her insecurities and . . . he was frowning. At *her*. Not at the disappearing back of the woman, but at *her*.

"Come in. Shut the door. Sit down," he said, motioning to a plush blue chair that faced the desk.

She did as he said, quickly and without a sound. She was used to anger and to being treated like a mouse. Her parents had been volatile people. Of course, she'd never before had so much riding on her behavior. . . .

The man gave her a long once-over. His gaze passed over her face to the pulse in her throat and down to where her hands were clamped on the arms of the chair. With some effort, she slowed her breathing and loosened her grip.

"You're Genevieve Patchett, I take it," he said. "All right, let's begin." But it was clear as the wall of windows behind him that he had no interest in beginning anything with her. He was still frowning.

Genevieve wanted to whimper. For the thousandth time since her world, her security, and all that was familiar to her had been stolen six months ago, she felt as if she was hanging over the edge of a cliff by her fingertips. And slipping. The fear inside her was like a living being. Her reputation was destroyed, and soon the last of her money, all that was left of her fortune after her ex-fiancé financial advisor had emptied most of her accounts, would be gone. Then she'd be reduced to sleeping on the streets. So running from the only job interview she'd been able to secure didn't appear to be an option. Lucas McDowell was either going to save her or eat her for lunch.

Stop it, she told herself. The man might have eyes with steel gates, he might be an industry giant, his recreational equipment company in the Fortune 500, but she had grown up in a family that was feted by the elite of the world. The fact that she was now reduced to scrambling for her next meal didn't change that. And her parents had always told her that attitude, or at least the pretense of it, could get a person anything.

"Mr. McDowell." She sat up very straight and tall and forced herself to ignore the unpleasant scenario with the woman she'd just witnessed. She did her best to stare straight into those intimidating silver-gray eyes. "I would like . . ."

"No," he said, his voice like a silken knife as he cut her off. "Ms. Patchett, we both know that what you would like isn't what's going to decide your fate today."

"My . . . fate?" The way he said it, as if he already had some sort of power over her when she'd walked in here of her own volition, made Genevieve feel ill. More alone than she already felt. Still, she'd been lucky that he'd granted her this audience, because the result of this interview would affect her a lot more than it would him. "Okay," she agreed, waiting for him to go on. The urge

10

to squirm under his insolent inspection was intense.

"Let's make one thing clear. The only reason you're here is that one of my employees just eloped to Australia and you've been recommended to me by Teresa March," he said, although Genevieve already knew that. It was a sheer stroke of luck that Teresa had been in town visiting relatives and mentioned that Lucas, a man Teresa had once worked for, was in Chicago looking for an assistant just when Genevieve was starting to count her last pennies. Teresa hadn't even hesitated. She'd insisted on trying to get Gen a job.

What should I say? Genevieve wondered. *Should I say anything? Should I tell him how grateful I am to Teresa? Will that make me look too desperate?* She didn't know. Despite being twenty-six, this was all virgin territory for her. Debutantes didn't have to worry about such things.

Go with your gut feelings, she thought, but doing that had made her trust Barry and enabled him to steal all her money and betray her, to hurt her. Still, Teresa might well have saved her life by getting her this interview. She deserved praise.

"Teresa is a saint," she said, then blushed when Lucas lifted one eyebrow. Teresa had a well-known reputation as a fun-loving party girl even if she was a very intelligent party girl who never let her fun get in the way of work.

"Well, she's not exactly a saint, but she's really a very nice person, once you get to know her," Genevieve corrected. "I . . . Of course you do know her and . . ."

Lucas's expression told her nothing. He simply waited as she grew more flustered.

Genevieve wanted to clap her hand over her mouth. Why was she babbling? Lucas McDowell clearly didn't consider her his dream candidate. Now, he was going to think that she had air for brains and send her away without a job!

"I'm incredibly grateful to her for getting this interview for me," she concluded somewhat lamely, then immediately wondered if that comment made her sound too pathetically eager.

Giving her a quick but very thorough glance, one that made her feel as if he could read her thoughts and see right down to the pale pink stripe on her underwear, he casually scribbled something on a notepad. Genevieve's heart started to pound more furiously than it already had been. She had a vision of herself spending her last dime and not knowing which way to turn or where to go.

"I'm sorry. I . . . Mr. McDowell, could we please start over?" she asked.

He put the pad down and came around the desk, leaning back against it and crossing his arms. Now he was close and so tall that Genevieve was forced to look up into those too perceptive eyes.

"Start over?"

"Yes. Like this. I'm Genevieve Patchett, I understand that you have a job to fill and I would very much like to be the person to do that job. I have references." She pulled out the list Teresa had helped her compose and held it out. The fact that those references were mostly from people who might not yet have heard all the evil rumors Barry had spread about her made her feel guilty. She wanted to ask Lucas not to believe any gossip he heard about her, but Teresa had warned her not to. Still, it was difficult to keep her mouth shut. Dishonesty, even by omission, didn't come naturally to her.

Lucas took the paper, his big hand just inches from hers. Her breath felt as if it was trapped in her chest as Lucas put the paper behind him on his desk without looking at it.

"You don't want them?" Her voice came out too breathless.

"I don't need them. I've already checked your background. I know all I need to know. If I hadn't checked you out beforehand, you wouldn't be here."

"I see," she said softly. But her mind was a whirl. What did he know? What had he heard? What hadn't he heard?

For the first time, Lucas smiled slightly. He was a rough-hewn man, but even that hint of a smile transformed his face into something . . . mesmerizingly male and virile. And dangerous. Genevieve realized she was trying to push back farther in her chair before she stopped herself and years of lessons in posture kicked in. She sat up even straighter, raised her chin higher. *Try to at least look confident and competent,* she ordered herself.

"You don't see," he said. "But that's not your fault. This job won't be exactly like anything you've done before."

She opened her mouth to tell him that she hadn't ever had a job, then closed it. He'd said that he knew her background. If that was true, then he undoubtedly knew that. But maybe he wanted to test her honesty. She opened her mouth again, then shut it once more. Honesty could lose this for her. And then she'd starve and then . . .

"I —" She closed her eyes, prepared to do

14

the right thing or at least hope that the words that came out of her mouth would be the right ones. It was still a matter of choosing truth over famine. A woman couldn't eat truth for breakfast.

"You've never had a real job before, have you?" he asked, ending her dilemma.

A wave of nausea swept over her. She swallowed hard. "Does it matter?" *Please say no. Please say no.*

"I don't know yet. It depends."

Her heart started pounding. This must have been what walking a tightrope over a roiling river felt like. There were so many mistakes a person could make, and any one of them would land her in the water.

Genevieve took a deep, shaky breath, hoping that the man didn't notice how nervous she was. "What — what does it depend on?"

"For starters, you don't have a clue what this job even entails yet, do you?"

"Not really." She hoped that it didn't entail anything too revolting or something that was beyond her abilities. "What do you want me to do?"

"What I want if you suit, if I give you the job . . . well, let's begin with a few questions about you."

Exasperating man. He hadn't answered her question and . . . oh, no, here came the tough part. *Don't ask me about the lies Barry spread about me, because I've already had too many people turn their backs on me because of that.*

"What do you consider to be your talents?"

Uh-oh, this felt like one of those questions that could get her thrown out the door before the interview had even begun. "I . . ." *Under less nerve-racking circumstances, I can make small talk, I know how to dress, how to choose a good wine, how to oversee servants.* Somehow she doubted that any of those were going to be of any assistance here. "I'm not sure exactly what kind of talent you're looking for," she said, stalling and hoping he would give her a hint that she could build on.

"Not really an answer, is it?" he said, catching her in the act. "All right. I need someone who knows how to make things happen."

Bad news, since the only things she'd made happen lately were bad things. She was not going to say that, she thought, feeling suddenly faint. *Don't keel over,* she ordered herself. *Just don't.*

"I've . . ." Her voice cracked. Somehow she managed to swallow, take a deep breath and start over. If she didn't come up with a

16

suitable answer now, if she didn't sound convincing, she was going to lose this chance. Genevieve struggled to keep breathing normally. "I've — I've organized . . . events and managed guest lists," she said, her voice coming out amazingly strong, given how frantically her heart was pounding. Okay, the event was merely a big society party her parents threw every year, and frankly, her part had never been that difficult. Her parents always told her exactly what they wanted and they always wanted the same thing. As for the guest list, people had always flocked to see her parents' art, so her main task had been whittling the list down to manageable proportions. Her role had always been a quiet one both in planning the party and in keeping records of her parents' work.

Lucas folded his arms over his chest, which only served to emphasize the breadth of his shoulders and made her feel even smaller than she was. A small smile lifted his lips. As if he knew what she was thinking. She hoped he didn't know what she was thinking.

"Your parents, Ann and Theo Patchett, certainly set the world on fire with their flair for design and their talent with stained and blown glass. I understand that you traveled

17

with them everywhere, were at their side at every event, and I imagine that you were born making things happen."

But he imagined wrong, Genevieve thought. Her parents had been personalities and she had learned how to do all the things they wanted, how to dress and walk and talk and smile and how to quietly live in the large shadow they cast, how to bolster their egos. There was nothing powerful about her. And in recent history, nothing wise. After her parents' deaths, she had been taken in by a con man, one her parents had adored and introduced her to. She had been engaged to that con man, robbed by him and dumped by him, too. She hadn't made things happen.

Apparently, Lucas McDowell thought otherwise. Should she tell him the truth?

No, you're good at following orders. Just . . . follow orders and try to do what he tells you. If he hires you, that is.

"Your parents decorated some of the most luxurious homes in the world," he was saying. "Teresa caught me just when I was going to begin interviewing candidates. I need someone who knows decorating and has organizational skills. I'm extremely interested in that kind of talent."

Genevieve wondered exactly what Teresa

had told Lucas and how well he actually knew Teresa. Teresa was a smart woman, no doubt she'd been a good employee, but she had no aversion to embellishing a story, either. If Lucas thought that Genevieve was a creative genius like her parents and if he found out the truth . . . Genevieve couldn't brazenly lie, not after what had happened with Barry. She opened her mouth to say that she was nothing like her parents, then shut it again. Wasn't there some way she could make this work out for both herself and Lucas?

"I don't have my parents' experience on a commercial level or . . . okay, on any level," she said truthfully, "but I *have* spent my whole life in beautiful rooms, admiring them, studying them for long hours, in some cases cataloguing the details when my parents wanted assistance." Which wasn't what he was looking for at all, she didn't think, but . . . he studied her closely.

She tried not to squirm or to think of him as a gorgeous man. That was so not relevant. Her trust had been betrayed many times in her life in small ways, but never so thoroughly as it had been with Barry. Love — being blinded by a man — had been her downfall. It wasn't happening again. Even if the incident with the beautiful brunette hadn't taken place, Teresa had already warned her that Lucas had a solid reputation as a fast-moving rolling stone and a heartbreaker who never really let his guard down with a woman. She'd also said that he was totally tempting, but she needn't have bothered.

It doesn't matter how astoundingly virile he is, Gen thought. She didn't want a man. Of any kind. All that she wanted right now was work. Money. Salvation. A new life where she would stand on her own two feet, order her own world and rely on no one. Trust no one. Love no one. Simple rules.

But first she had to get the job. She looked up to find Lucas studying her closely.

"Who chose your outfit?" he suddenly asked.

"Excuse me?" She blinked and lurched in her chair, but she quickly regained her calm expression. What an odd question, but . . . so what? Maybe he was just some sort of eccentric. As long as he wasn't a lecher or an ax murderer — and she'd never read anything that indicated that he was either of those — nothing else mattered beyond the fact that he had a job that needed filling.

"I chose it." Okay, she'd had it made. She'd had plenty of money at the time.

"Hmm."

Genevieve tried to keep from responding to that. And lost the battle. "Is that a bad 'hmm'?"

"It's an interested one." He looked at her bronze skirt and dark gold blouse with the small, cream-colored star-shaped glass buttons she'd made herself, each one slightly asymmetrical and different from the next. "The effect is muted, tasteful, in some ways even a bit old-fashioned." Which was right. This was one of the oldest outfits she had. "But the buttons are . . . most unusual. They're a bit out of step with the rest of your attire, but in spite of being a bit unconventional, they work. It's an outfit, not a room that needs decorating, but the skills are related. You know about color and planning and how to mix things up so that the big picture works. And the colors complement your red hair."

Genevieve was grateful that he hadn't used the word *fiery*. Her parents hadn't cared for her hair's particular shade of red and had tried to get her to dye it many times. Barry had hated it, preferring blondes. Or at least preferring the blonde he'd spent Genevieve's money on. In her one act of defiance she'd kept the color but had toned things down by pulling her hair back and out of the way in a severe ponytail that made her hair less noticeable. Or so she'd hoped.

"The skirt is too short, though," Lucas said suddenly, and automatically Genevieve looked down to her crossed legs. The skirt exposed her knees and a bit more.

She bit her lip.

"Say it," he said.

"I'm . . . sorry," she said, although she wasn't sorry. She was chagrined. Lucas was either not going to hire her or he was going to be very difficult to work for. "I . . . this is the length I usually wear my skirts. Will this be a problem with your dress code?"

Lucas looked amused. "I don't have one. I just wanted to know if you would defend your choice."

"I —" She wanted to tell him that he was being unfair. She was interviewing and was afraid to argue with a potential employer. But telling someone they were being unfair wasn't her style. She was the "go along to get along" type. And right now she was scared and nervous and tired and hungry.

"I wish you wouldn't play games with me," she said, surprising herself. Maybe she was more tired than she'd realized, because she was definitely acting stupid. What man would hire someone who reprimanded him? She opened her mouth to apologize.

Too late. Lucas was already speaking. "You're right. My comment was unfair, given the circumstances. So, let's just do this. For the rest of this interview, you try turning off the nerves and act exactly the way you would if you were already working for me. All right?"

"And . . ." She swallowed hard. "That is . . . what if you don't like the way I act?"

He shrugged. "I won't hire you. The minute I have an inkling of doubt I'll end the interview. Is that fair?"

It was terrifying. "Are you always this frank, Mr. McDowell?" If he hired her, would she be on full alert every hour she was on the job?

"Always."

He stared directly into her eyes, and she couldn't look away. That intense expression of his . . . she felt as if he was daring her to object to his tactics. Genevieve's body began to hum with awareness. This man was very potent, and the fact that he held her future in his hands was very scary, but she had told herself that she preferred truth to deception and just because that truth was unnerving wasn't necessarily a bad thing. Because Lucas McDowell hadn't ended the interview yet. She still had a chance to get back on to solid ground.

"I think . . . I'm good with all this, Mr. McDowell. You're being fair."

"I'm being a bit of a jerk, and your skirt's just fine."

It was. It was perfectly decent. Even so, Genevieve was suddenly aware of her knees in a way she'd never been aware in her life. She was very conscious of the fact that Lucas McDowell had been studying her legs. Even though he had shown no interest whatsoever.

"Okay," she said.

He looked as if he was going to smile, but . . . not quite. "Okay, that I'm a jerk or that your skirt fits the bill?"

"I —"

He shook his head. "Never mind. Don't answer that. Answer this, instead. Do you have any strong feelings about the homeless, about people who have no money or prestige, people who may have been in trouble?"

I'm seriously going to faint, she thought. *Is he talking about me? How much research did he do? Does he know everything about my situation?*

"I think . . . that people shouldn't be judged by their financial situations. I would hope that most people felt that way." Even though she knew that that wasn't the case.

24

Lucas nodded. "All right. Last question. You and Teresa haven't seen much of each other since you've grown up, but when you were young, you were close, she tells me. I'm sure she shared secrets with you. I make it my business to know everything about my employees past and present. Can you tell me some of those secrets?"

"No!" Genevieve's voice came out a bit too loud, but shock at the bizarre and rude question rushed through her. For a moment she felt physically ill. Maybe she'd never interviewed for a job before, but she was sure that such questions were out of line and just plain alarming. What kind of man was this?

She looked up at Lucas and knew that in that moment, with that *no,* she had sealed her fate. The sick feeling grew. Lucas was gazing at her intently, waiting, those gray eyes mesmerizing. Hard. Cold. Demanding. What would it be like to have no money, no home, no food? No doubt she was about to find out.

"No," she said again, softly this time. Teresa, despite her playful attitude and her money, had had a harsh childhood. She trusted Genevieve. "No."

Lucas's cold gray gaze softened, just a

touch. "When can you begin work?" he asked.

"What?"

"Work. When can you begin work? That's what you came for, isn't it?"

"Yes, but I thought — your question . . . I . . ."

"Most people have a few dark secrets in their closet. I have no interest in prying into Teresa's past. What I needed to know was whether you would spill those secrets in order to get a job. That's all I needed to ascertain."

His deep voice delivering the news she most needed to hear seemed to rumble right through her body, touching every nerve ending on its journey. Genevieve let out a deep, shaky breath, still disoriented and more than a little alarmed by her physical attraction to this man when he was so obviously someone who didn't play by the rules. She had been fooled by people reputed to be straight shooters. How on earth could she deal with someone whose methods she couldn't even begin to understand?

"I'm afraid that you have me at a disadvantage, Mr. McDowell. Teresa told me that the job might involve a little decorating, some clerical or organizational skills. She told me what little she knew, but . . . as I mentioned earlier, I have no real idea what the job will entail or why you would need to know whether I would spill my guts about a friend's past."

"I know, and I apologize for the bizarre nature of this interview. My only rationale is that the work you'll be doing, should you accept the task, is in some ways very public, but other parts are very sensitive. The person I hire has to be capable of dealing with sensitive personal information, but it's difficult to measure that kind of loyalty. Most job candidates would insist that they were capable of discretion, but in reality not that many can resist retelling a juicy story. So, my apologies for my methods. I guarantee that from here on out, we'll have the most practical and ordinary of business relationships."

Genevieve highly doubted that. There was nothing ordinary about Lucas McDowell. "All right," she said. "Can you tell me what the job is now, please?"

He looked slightly amused.

"What?"

"You're exceptionally polite, given the fact that I no doubt creeped you out."

She tilted her head. "You hold the cards."

"So I do. All right, Genevieve, I've bought a large piece of property in the suburbs. The

27

plan is to create a shelter for women who are down on their luck, a place to rebuild the lives of those who've been damaged by poverty or circumstances. We're going to make it something the city can be proud of. I'm hoping it will spawn other such establishments, so we're going to give it plenty of publicity. I want Angie's House to be a perfect jewel, a success that will be the epicenter of a growing movement that will change lives. That means lots of buzz in order to jump-start the project with the public and potential sponsors of future Angie's Houses.

"However, once we open the doors, we can't forget that the women who'll live there have already been betrayed by life. Some of them will want to keep the more personal aspects of their hardships to themselves. Others may put their trust in you by sharing parts of their stories. It's important that whoever I hire knows how to put on a big show but also how to keep a confidence. I have to know that whoever works with me will talk up the concept while never betraying the trust of the prospective new tenants. It's a fine line we'll be walking."

Genevieve knew what it was like to have her trust betrayed. She shuddered.

"That's why you asked me about Teresa."

"If you had tried to say one word about her past, I would have stopped you. And I couldn't have hired you."

She looked up into Lucas's harsh face. "Mr. McDowell, I assure you that I understand. It isn't always easy or smart to trust someone. Words aren't enough."

"Agreed."

"So . . . why me?" she asked.

He shrugged. "I choose my employees carefully. Teresa is trustworthy. She recommended you. That alone wouldn't have been enough, however. I need a good project manager and I'm sure I could have found someone else. You, however, have an edge."

For the job of project manager? Genevieve wanted to close her eyes. Had Teresa overstated her skills? Did Lucas McDowell think she knew more than she did?

"What's my edge?" she managed to ask.

"If you've organized your parents' society events, you have a handle on how to make things happen and how to deal with time constraints, problems, setbacks and personnel. You've proven that you can keep a secret should that become necessary, and you have some experience with decor, something I lack. Furthermore, and most importantly, because as I said, I don't want this project, Angie's House, to be a single entity, you have the name to get people talking, to attract the kind of attention we need to bring in other donors for other houses."

Genevieve struggled to keep her hands from shaking. The last thing she wanted right now was attention. The last thing she was capable of was bringing in people on the mere mention of her name.

She tried to swallow, struggled to find her voice. "*You* have a famous name."

He shook his head. "I have money and a successful business. With a few exceptions, famous entrepreneurs don't become household names. But people like your parents? World renowned artists? Yes, they do. Their name is like a glowing diamond. It puts people in a good mood, gets them excited. And you happen to share it."

Genevieve's heart fell a bit. Her importance hinged on her parents' talents as it always had. She wanted to back away. But she couldn't afford to.

"Does that mean I really do have the job?" She managed to ask.

"If you want it."

She wanted it, but she must have been slow to say yes.

"If you don't, tell me now. I'm on a strict timeline. I have another job waiting in France when this one is done, an opening of a new store in Japan after that and I intend to finish up here in six weeks. So, if you can't do this, Genevieve, or if you don't want to, tell me. You're free to go."

She *wanted* to walk away. There were things she didn't like about this setup. *Her* name, unlike her parents' names, would be of no use. She should tell Lucas that. She didn't really even have the skills he needed. And then there was the man, this intimidating, far too masculine man. But . . . hunger gnawed at her. Her faintness wasn't only from nerves. She wasn't free. She had to have this.

"I'd like the job, please," she said. "I'll be your . . ."

"Project manager."

She nodded. The title was that belonging to a bolder person, one who knew how to take charge of situations and not be tricked or bullied into doing things she didn't want to do.

"I'll be your project manager. I'm your woman."

For a moment, those gray eyes turned fierce. Genevieve realized just how little she knew about this man.

"Good." Lucas held out his hand, and Genevieve automatically reached out. His fingers closed around hers, his hand much larger than hers. She should have felt trapped, insignificant. Instead, as heat seeped from his skin to hers, she was suddenly aware of him as a man more than as her new boss. That could be a problem if she let it. She wouldn't.

"You should know that I believe in being hands-on in a project like this, Genevieve," he said, releasing her. "If you and I are going to oversee and sell this project, we have to know it from the ground up. Every higher level employee at every factory and store I own spent some time in the trenches so that they could fully understand the business, so we'll get started on your ground-floor experience right away. I'll pick you up tomorrow. We're headed straight for Angie's House. Dress for work."

"What kind?"

"The dirty kind. Do you have clothing you can mess up?"

She had clothing. It was the one thing she still had in abundance. Whether or not she had what Lucas meant, however, was questionable.

"No problem," she said, hoping her smile was reassuring. "Let me give you my address."

"I have it already."

Once again, Genevieve had that feeling of

being overwhelmed, too small and insignificant next to this man. She felt vulnerable, and vulnerable was the last thing she wanted or needed to feel right now.

"I won't let you get to me, Mr. McDowell," she muttered to herself later when she scoured her closet looking for something that could rightfully be called work clothes.

But she knew she lied. The man seemed to know everything about her. He felt like a powerful dark tornado that drops out of the sky, wreaks havoc in your life and then roars off again. He had her at a disadvantage, and she had sworn she would never be at a disadvantage with a man again. She would have to work on that and just start ignoring all the unnerving things about Lucas. She hoped that was possible.

Lucas shook his head after Genevieve was gone. This might well be a disaster in the making. She was young, destitute and had never worked at a job in her life. Despite her telling him that she wanted the job, she might change her mind later if there were complications or strife or if something better came along. He'd spent most of his youth dealing with people who thought they wanted to do something good but later changed their minds when things hit a rough patch.

What's more, she was far too pretty. Even with her hair scraped back from her face so brutally, or maybe because of it, her classic features were striking. And also . . . a vision of her legs and those luscious knees crept in, and he quickly slapped that right out of his consciousness. The last thing he needed was to get involved with a socialite who was down on her luck and looking to improve her situation. Women . . . and others had used him or tried to use him before. Repeatedly. As an orphan in the foster system, people had thought taking him in would earn them Good Samaritan points. As a man who'd fought his way to wealth and power, women like Rita thought he'd make a nice trophy or else they wanted his money and power. The only thing that none of them realized was that he had nothing to give them, emotionally or any other way. He'd spent all his emotional capital years ago, wasted it, burnt it, lost it. Now all he had — all he would ever allow himself — was work and guilt.

But he was not going to feel guilty about Genevieve Patchett. Their relationship would be work only, nothing personal. He wasn't responsible for her problems, and she wasn't going to be on his conscience.

And he wasn't going to think about her legs, either, or those gorgeous green eyes. At least not much.

CHAPTER TWO

The next morning, Genevieve crawled from bed and faced the dirty, cracked and chalky walls of the small room she had rented.

Today is the day I start working for Lucas McDowell, she thought, trying to choke back the fear that accompanied the thought. Would she be able to be the kind of employee that Lucas wanted? She'd never even needed to work before. But now . . .

"I need —"

Her words were interrupted by an angry shout echoing through the paper-thin walls. Something hard hit the wall. Caught off guard, Genevieve jumped. Even though such sounds weren't at all unusual, she had yet to get used to how close and heated everything was. How desperate. How different from the life of luxury that was all she'd known until a few months ago. Tension coiled within her. That old life was gone. It wasn't just this place that seemed desper-

36

ate. *She* was desperate.

The tension slid up a notch as, once again, the reality of her situation hit home. The sun had already risen and Genevieve knew that anytime now, her landlady might appear, screeching, demanding the rent that Gen didn't have. Threatening.

Before now, no one had ever seriously threatened her in her entire life.

But Mrs. Dohenny would, and she had the right to do that. Genevieve was a full month behind on her rent. She fought the sickness that followed that thought and tried to rush. She hoped to be gone long before Mrs. Dohenny showed up. The last thing she needed was for her new boss to find out that she was, essentially, living here without paying. Gen remembered her father yelling at a doorman who had displeased him in some way. Firing the man as he pleaded for his job so that he could feed his family. Ignoring the man's pleas.

"Stop it," she whispered weakly. *Don't think about that. It's not helping.* She didn't even know why she was thinking about that incident now.

No, that was a lie. She knew. She was afraid of failing, of becoming the doorman and having Lucas fire her on her first day.

Closing her eyes for a second, she dragged

in a deep, shaky breath and tried to proceed with her tasks. Quickly, she showered in the small, cramped tub with its leaking, rusty showerhead and broken, institution-green plastic tiles, exited the bathroom and moved to the battered three-legged dresser that was the only piece of furniture other than the bed and one wooden chair.

Her reflection in the cracked mirror above the dresser was too pale, the meager items on it a sad testimony to how far she had fallen. An almost empty jar of expensive cleansing cream shared space with half a tube of lipstick in a golden, emerald-studded case and a tiny half-used vial of perfume she refused to touch except in emergencies, because it felt like armor, the last little bit she possessed. Once it was gone, there would be no more.

Staring at these remnants of her past life, Genevieve sighed. The cost of these three items new would have paid her rent in this little broom closet of a room several times over, but now they were merely some of the last precious remnants of a lifestyle she'd never, ever know again.

The cheap clock clicked loudly as another minute passed. Genevieve looked at the sagging mattress so unlike the luxuriously soft bed encased in crisp scented sheets she'd once had, and a drumbeat of panic began to pound in her breast. Lucas McDowell was picking her up soon. What if he saw this room with its holes in the plaster and the windows that had bars over them to keep the bad people out? Then he would know that she couldn't even take care of herself, much less be a project manager.

She couldn't let that happen. She grabbed the lipstick with shaky fingers and gathered the few other items. Carefully, sparingly, trying to make these last remnants of her once elegant life last a bit longer, she began to apply her makeup. Then, she picked out the most casual clothing she could find. When Lucas got here, she would need to find a smile and something that looked like confidence. Not for the first time in her life, she wished that she was the outgoing, confident type who won people with her dazzling personality and talent instead of being the quiet, behind-the-scenes type.

But wishing had never made anything happen in her life. It hadn't made her parents love her. It hadn't saved her from her con-man financial-advisor fiancé. All she had to help her right now was the determination to do whatever she had to in order to survive.

No, more than survive, she hoped. She

wanted to be . . . more, to become a different person: bolder, more successful, independent. Make that completely, totally, "never rely or lean on anyone again in her life" independent.

That meant she had to please Lucas McDowell.

No matter what.

Lucas frowned as he pulled up in front of the dark, ugly apartment building that matched the address he had for Genevieve Patchett. He wasn't a native to Chicago, but he'd lived here for a while as a teenager; he'd done business in this city on numerous occasions, and even if he hadn't, he knew a bad neighborhood when he saw one. As a child he'd lived in them, nearly died in them, and this one had "get out of here if you can" written all over it. He'd recognized that before he'd gotten within three blocks of this place. This wasn't your standard debutante living arrangement.

Genevieve had fallen even further than he'd guessed. But then, that wasn't his problem, was it? His new project manager's abode wasn't any of his business. The only reason he was here at all was to escort her to the work site, and he wouldn't even be doing that except for the fact that summer construction had temporarily disrupted public transportation to the area where Angie's House was located.

So ignore this place. Just go get her, he told himself, reaching for the car door handle.

At that moment he saw her. She exited the building like a rabbit being chased by a fox, zipping out the door, glancing back over her shoulder with fear in her eyes.

Yeah, that was fear. He was familiar with the expression. Something had Genevieve Patchett spooked.

"No, please don't get out," she said, hurrying to the passenger side of his black sports car. "I — I don't want to be late on my first day and . . . and someone might hurt your car if you leave it."

She reached for the handle, practically dove for the thing.

He exited the car, ignoring her fluttering and flustered admonitions. Despite the fact that she was none of his concern, there were rules to be followed. Rules and discipline kept a person safe and helped maintain distance. They kept things under control, and being in control was . . . necessary. It had always been of supreme importance ever since he finally — thank the stars — realized that he didn't have to be at the mercy of others' damaging, self-serving whims. So . . .

"I'm not that worried about the car, Gene-vieve." Without another word, he moved to the passenger door and opened it for her. But as they drove away, and despite himself, he couldn't help wondering what it was that she was so afraid of.

And that kind of speculation would have to stop. He had no business thinking any-thing about Genevieve Patchett beyond the tasks they would share. He liked his world well-ordered — by him — and already he could see that she, with those vulnerable green eyes that betrayed her every emotion, would create the kind of havoc that he never allowed in his life. He didn't get deeply involved. With anyone. Certainly not with his employees, so it was a good thing that she was here to do a job and a short-term job at that. Their paths would only run parallel for a very brief period of time.

Then he would never think about her ever again. Which was a very good thing, he reminded himself.

Still, for the moment, she was here, she was his employee. That alone made her his responsibility, and . . . she was wearing some pale blue lacy thing. A blouse. With pencil-slim light-colored pants. Shoes with a little heel. Very stylish. No doubt very expensive, but not the kind of thing that would survive the day ahead.

He couldn't hold back a frown. How had he let Teresa talk him into this, he thought, then reminded himself that he was the one who had hired Genevieve, not Teresa. *Because Genevieve is a Patchett,* he told himself. *Because she has the required skills and a name that may prove useful.* Having her name attached to this project would engender the kind of attention and cachet that was needed to make Angie's House the next big "it" charity. It would get Angie's House in the newspapers, so how Genevieve looked to him was unimportant.

Which was a good thing, because right now, he thought, glancing to the side, she looked very good. Those clothes might be impractical but they fit her curves to perfection. Her pink mouth looked very . . .

Small. Pink. Moist.

Darn it, McDowell, stop it. She's off-limits. "Is that the plainest thing you have?" he asked, scattering all those inappropriate thoughts he was having.

She fidgeted with the door handle in what looked to be a nervous reaction. "I'm sorry. It was the only thing I had that was cotton."

"Silk and satin more your thing?" He

frowned again.

Genevieve took a deep breath. "I . . . I hadn't anticipated all of this."

He wasn't sure what "all of this" entailed but she suddenly seemed even more vulnerable than she had before. He wondered once again at the wisdom of hiring her. Could she handle this job?

"I told you about how all my employees get involved on the ground floor, but I didn't explain how monumental this task is. The building where Angie's House will be located is a total mess. I'm afraid your clothes are going to get pretty dirty."

She gave a small nod, as if she was used to being handed bad news. And he guessed she was of late, given that her money was all gone.

"If my clothes get dirty, then I'll wash them," she said in a small, quiet voice. "I need to learn to do things like that. I'm not afraid of work, Mr. McDowell."

Maybe she believed that, but she hadn't seen the inside of this place yet. Her hands were pale cream, soft. Hands that didn't do manual labor or come into contact with dirt on any kind of a regular basis. And the mere fact that she was *learning* how to do things like wash a blouse practically screamed "privileged." Unlike her, he hadn't been

44

born to wealth, even if he had plenty of money now. He knew how to use his hands, and with the tight schedule he'd set for the completion of this project, he didn't have time to baby her.

This was a deadline that couldn't be missed . . . for numerous reasons. The opening date was significant in ways he preferred not to think about, but there was also the fact that delaying things would result in innocent, needy people waiting longer for their chance to move in. Those people had no money and never had. There wasn't a soft-skinned, lace-and-satin princess in the bunch.

"I don't have time to baby you," he said as if his brain had somehow foolishly directed him to say what he was thinking. Or maybe because a part of him hoped that if he was callous with her, he would stop wanting another glimpse of those big green eyes.

"I assure you that I don't need special treatment." But despite the softness of her voice, he could tell that he had offended her. That was unprofessional of him. It was unacceptable. Getting personal with his employees for good or for ill was not allowed.

"What do you need?" he asked.

A slight tremble visibly rippled through

her delicate frame. She seemed to consider her words carefully. "Honesty — that is, I would be happy for simple, honest work."

So she'd started to tell him she needed honesty, then had probably decided that it was the wrong thing to say to her boss. The obvious response was to simply tell her that he would be honest with her. But he wasn't going to say that. He had learned long ago to do what was necessary, and what was necessary wasn't always honest or pretty. He had been raised in a harsh world of broken promises, so the only promises he made were of the most limited variety.

"You'll have honest work and I'll pay you well for it," he said. It was, after all, all that he had to offer anyone.

"Thank you, Mr. McDowell."

The weariness in her soft voice made him feel like a jerk. The relationship already felt strained, and that was a problem. For the next few weeks, they would be working together and they would need to work quickly. He needed her cooperation. He needed her *not* to call him Mr. McDowell, but he couldn't for the life of him figure out why. Maybe he didn't want to know why.

"Just Lucas."

"Lucas, then. I may not have been raised to be self-sufficient, but I intend to learn how to be totally independent. I *have* to be independent, to know that I can rely on myself to do it all. I want that more than anything. So, there's no cheating allowed. No shortcuts such as looking for someone to marry, support or save me. I need to become totally self-sufficient, to do this and do it well, so don't worry about the blouse."

She smiled, a bit uncertainly, and he couldn't help but be affected by those tell-all-her-secrets eyes and her naïveté. She had no clue what she was doing, but she was going to do it. Her determination when the odds were stacked against her made him want to learn more about her, and that wasn't allowed. He didn't get involved with anyone and especially not with someone like Genevieve. Because despite, or maybe because of, his association with Angie's House and the situation that had driven him to take on this project, vulnerable women were poison to his soul, a reminder of times he wanted to forget. That wasn't going to change.

Genevieve quickly scrambled to exit the car. She didn't want Lucas thinking she expected him to open her door or give her any special favors.

Still, when he threw open the door of the

house, she had to fight not to exclaim. The entryway was huge, and while there was very little furniture, what was there was absolutely caked in dust and dirt. Cobwebs hung everywhere, and the few cobwebs she had ever encountered in her life prior to this had sent chills running up her spine. In addition, there was plaster scattered over the filthy floor where part of the chandelier had come loose and pulled part of the ceiling with it. The windows were grimy.

"How long has this been empty?" she couldn't help asking. "And why?"

"Years. It was originally a smaller house, enlarged and then enlarged again by a man who won the lottery, then lost all his money at a dizzying speed. It's too big and costly for the rest of the neighborhood, not in a good enough location for anyone who could afford it. So, it sat here, unwanted and out of place for years, ever since he walked away from it. No one knew what to do with it."

Something cold and steel-like in the way he had said "unwanted and out of place" made Genevieve turn to look at him, but his expression gave nothing away.

"Why . . . I don't understand. Why would you choose it, then?"

The smallest of smiles lifted his lips. Far from making him look less dangerous, it

48

made him seem more handsome. The flutter it brought to her stomach practically screamed "step away from the gorgeous man, Gen. This one will hurt you."

"I'm sorry. Did I say something funny? Or wrong?" she asked.

Lucas stared directly into her eyes, pinning her so that she felt powerless to look away. The flutter intensified. She almost backed up a step to try to curb her too-feminine reaction to him. "I suppose I'm not used to hiring members of the privileged class," he said. "Most employees steer away from questioning my motives."

Uh-oh. Her lack of experience was showing. "I shouldn't have asked," she observed.

"No. Ask what you want to know. I'll answer if I feel it's pertinent to the project. In this case, you're dead-on. We needed a big building, but not one that would attract a lot of attention. Tucked away in this low-income but solid and safe residential area, the women of Angie's House won't stand out. They can move around in safety, become members of the community and, for once in their lives, have a place where they can — hopefully — heal and find some joy and satisfaction, unfettered by fear. The building suits our needs perfectly. Come on. I'll show you around."

She wanted to say no. There was something so empty and sad about the house. The fact that someone had built it during a happy time in their life and then lost all that happiness hit far too close to home. *But my misfortune was partly my own fault,* she reminded herself. The signs about Barry had been there, but she had ignored them. There had been times during their engagement when Barry had seemed shallow or uncaring of others and she had ignored it because her parents had liked him, her friends had admired him, and some of that admiration seemed to rub off on her.

Plus, while Barry had turned out to be a first-class jerk who had stolen much of her fortune while she'd been mourning the loss of her parents, the truth was that she'd had years before that to educate herself about her finances and she hadn't bothered to make the slightest effort. Even if she'd thought about questioning what Barry was doing, she wouldn't have known what questions to ask. If she'd known more, she might have saved herself, but now it was too late. The damage was done. There was no going back.

That was a good thing in only one way. She'd been forced to her knees and she wouldn't make the mistake of relying on anyone that way ever again.

"Lead on," she said, mustering some bravado. "I'm ready." *For anything.* But that last thought was a total lie. If Lucas smiled again and the hard line of his mouth softened again . . . well, now Genevieve finally understood what Teresa had meant when she fretted that Lucas might be too dangerous for her friend. She'd just been admonishing herself for being too trusting with one man and here she was staring at Lucas's mouth when he was a man who was obviously, glaringly someone she had no business thinking about at all beyond the job.

So stick to business, she told herself. *Try to figure out what's required and do a good job.* Otherwise, Lucas would have no reason to keep her. She would be cast aside by one more man.

She couldn't let that happen. From now on, she was going to throw herself into this project with every ounce of her being. Down that road lay freedom, redemption, independence. "I can't wait to get started," she said.

Lucas raised one dark brow.

"I mean it," Genevieve said. She needed to earn her first money, pay her overdue bills, prove herself and reclaim her self-respect.

Closing her eyes to her lack of experience,

51

she tried not to panic at the thought of the massive task ahead. "Where should I begin?" She glanced toward the brooms and rags and cleaning supplies in one corner.

"Today we'll just get you acclimated. I want you to get a feel for the building and the possibilities, what we need to accomplish. In time, there will be eight women living here, so you'll want to get a sense of the space and help me decide what we're going to do with it decorating and usage-wise. I deal in sporting goods and making money and I've spearheaded the construction of a number of stores, but I'm sure you'll have more of an idea about what women might want or need in a dream home. You're also the expert in decorating and events planning."

"Okay. So . . . what type of events will those be?" Her heart was pounding so hard she was amazed Lucas couldn't hear it. She had always been the behind-the-scenes person, not the up-front person.

"This house is in a residential neighborhood. We'll want to make sure the locals are comfortable with us. For that, we'll need to court them, to reassure them that the women here will be their neighbors, women committed to making life and this neighborhood a better place. This place —" he swung his arm out in an arc "— as I mentioned, is meant to be a place where women arrive broken and leave whole, with pride in who they are and who they can become."

Genevieve couldn't help herself then. "That's wonderful. What you're doing is wonderful." She couldn't help wondering what had sparked this project, but she didn't dare ask. Maybe she was clueless about a lot of things, but something so far-removed from the realm of running the sporting goods empire Lucas had built his reputation on? It had to be personal.

To her surprise, he frowned at her compliment. "*Wonderful* is a very strong word. It doesn't fit here. The fact is that I'm a very rich man, and I can get this started, but that's not nearly enough. The real power lies in getting other people, lots of other people, behind Angie's House and the next Angie's House and the next. So when we're done with the renovation, we'll open the doors. I want you to plan and oversee a major open house for the most elite members of the city. Our goal is to impress them and to impress *upon* them the need to get involved. Finally, you'll help me find the women who'll live here and the employees who'll work here."

She blinked, trying not to be overwhelmed, trying not to panic at what was going to be expected of her. *Breathe, Gen, breathe. Take it easy. Take it one step at a time,* she thought. *Just take one tiny step.* "Okay. That all makes sense. For now, I guess — I should probably get started on the cleaning. There's a lot of building here." *A whole lot of scrubbing for a woman who had never done anything like that.*

There was that elusive hint of a smile again, the straight, hard line of his mouth barely curving up at one corner. What had she said that was so amusing?

"I'm sure this isn't what you grew up doing and I don't expect you to single-handedly tackle this mess. I have two helpers coming in. They'll be assisting you as the project progresses and they'll be doing most of the repairing, painting and cleanup. But they'll respect you more if they see that you're not afraid of getting a little dirt beneath your fingernails."

Was that a dare? Genevieve had no idea and no real idea of how to begin. She wasn't even sure how to make use of her helpers who would be coming soon. She'd never been in this kind of position, and her parents had been flighty, self-absorbed people who probably weren't typical employers, so there was little use in trying to utilize her past experiences. Still, she didn't want to ask too many questions. If she was supposed to be a project manager, shouldn't she appear . . . managerial? She especially didn't want to ask anything that would make her look foolish. Barry had often made fun of her naïveté.

"All right. That makes sense. And I'm not afraid." Not of getting dirt under her finger-nails, but of Lucas, a man who overwhelmed by his presence and his manner and his looks . . . ? Yes, she was afraid, but she didn't want to think about that.

Instead, she picked up a broom and began to sweep. With vigor and determination. Soon the dust was swirling, flying all around, clogging her throat.

She couldn't hold back a cough.

Lucas appeared at her side. He touched her hand. Just the lightest of touches, but when his flesh met hers, fierce heat swirled through her, her breath caught, her whole body became aware of him as a man. She jerked back, stopped sweeping.

"Easy, Genevieve. It's just dust. You want to push it, not attack it. Like this." He demonstrated.

She took back the broom, embarrassed that she couldn't even manage the simplest of tasks. With some effort, she tried not to think about how Lucas's fingertips had felt against her skin.

It couldn't matter. Nothing could matter except succeeding. Moving on. Moving up. Learning. And getting good at being alone.

A mere two hours into the day, Lucas looked up to see that Genevieve was soaked to the skin. She was a total mess.

A beautiful mess, he corrected, then frowned at the thought. She was washing walls and water was sluicing down her arms, slicking away the layers of dirt she'd accumulated dusting and sweeping. The moisture turned her creamy skin shiny and damp and then sloshed onto her pale blue blouse, making it cling to her body.

But she wasn't complaining.

A sliver of admiration slipped through him followed by something else. Something hot when he stared at that damp fabric encasing her slender form.

Knock it off, McDowell. She's your employee. Your very temporary employee. And off-limits. In all ways.

Stifling a growl, Lucas threw down the cloth he was using to wash windows and went into the closet, where he had stashed a few changes of clothing. Removing a faded chambray shirt from a hanger, he walked over to Genevieve. "You might want this. And . . . you probably don't need to use that much water."

She looked up at him through dazed eyes. Tired eyes. He realized that she'd been working like a dog since she arrived two hours ago. When she looked at the shirt and then glanced down at her chest, he could see the jolt of embarrassment rip through her. That creamy skin turned almost as rosy as her hair.

"I — thank you. Yes, less water. I'll remember that," she said as she hastily reached out, took the shirt and slipped into it. It was miles too big for her. Baggy. Good.

"Time for a break," he said.

"No, I . . . I'm fine. I need to get this done. We're on a tight schedule, right?"

"We are. But even bosses need breathers. Thomas and Jorge will be here any minute. They'll need us to give them orders, to guide them. A boss that looks beat-up doesn't instill confidence in the employees." Which was true but sounded like a made-up excuse. Still, she gave him a tentative nod. She stopped long enough to have a drink of water and rest for a minute. Then she went back to her wall-washing.

When Thomas and Jorge showed up, Lucas introduced them. Thomas bowed slightly. "You are . . . *muy bonita,* Ms. Patchett," he said.

Jorge elbowed Thomas in the stomach. "Thomas, Ms. Patchett is our boss. Show some respect. Forgive my brother, Ms. Patchett. This is his first job."

To Lucas's surprise, Genevieve laughed. "There's nothing to forgive, Jorge. This is my —"

Uh-oh, the princess was going to tell Thomas and Jorge this was her first job, wasn't she? That would be a mistake.

Lucas coughed and glowered at her.

Her eyes widened and she looked at him. A flush climbed from the neck of his shirt to her cheeks. She turned back to Jorge. "I'm very pleased to meet you, Jorge. And Thomas, thank you so much for the compliment. I'm wet and dirty and I appreciate your efforts to make me feel better about that. I look forward to working with both of you." Wiping her palm on her pants, she held out her hand. The pink polish that had graced her nails this morning was chipped and her nails were ragged, but Thomas took her hand and bowed over it as if she were royalty. Jorge gave her a big smile and did the same.

Lucas had met the men before. He'd hired them, and Jorge had worked on a previous job. Now he said hello . . . and waited for his project manager to make the next move. When she said nothing, he glanced her way.

Genevieve stared him directly in the eyes, that pink glow growing rosier. Then she raised her chin and cleared her throat. "Lucas and I have been concentrating on cleaning the living room and entranceway. Thomas, why don't you work on the kitchen, and Jorge, take the family room. Let me know if you have any questions or concerns."

"I have a question. Will there be plaster work required? I have some experience in that area, but Thomas has none. If there's a lot of it to handle, we might need help."

A brief look of panic sprang into Genevieve's eyes. Lucas inwardly cursed, then opened his mouth to bail her out. But she was shaking her head. "I'm not sure yet. Let me get back to you on that. For now, let's just concentrate on getting rid of all the dirt."

The two men nodded, then wandered off. When they had gone, Lucas turned to her. "Good save."

She stared up at him with big eyes. "It was all I could think of. I don't know anything about plaster work."

"You know what a smooth wall looks like.

59

Jorge knows enough to handle any problem areas. There are a few but not much. I'll take you on a tour. We'll discuss what basic repair needs to be done. I should have done that already." Except a part of him had needed to see how "the debutante" handled the tough, dirty stuff. To his surprise, she was handling it. Not with any finesse, but with determination.

"Let's go," he said.

He led her through the rooms, pointing out problem areas, the general plan for cleanup, repair and renovation and the big picture. "When we're done, each woman will need her own private space but there needs to be plenty of flow and room for interaction. This is a house, but it will also be a community, hopefully a family. The space needs to reflect that."

Genevieve didn't say much, but she listened. She nodded. "And I'll be overseeing all of this."

Her voice sounded slightly faint.

Lucas frowned. "I'll work with you closely, but I have a business to run, other irons in the fire. This will largely be your project." Except he would personally see to it that the deadline didn't fall through. The deadline was that important.

"All right. I see." Genevieve gave a tight

nod. They turned down a hallway, not speaking, their steps silent on the carpeting.

The slosh of water sounded in a nearby room. "I don't know. Ms. Patchett is very nice, but . . . not experienced," Jorge was saying. "I hope she knows what she's doing and doesn't lead us into any mistakes. I don't want to lose this job."

"She's very pretty. Do you think she and Mr. McDowell . . . ?" Thomas's voice trailed off.

"Idiot. No," Jorge said. "I've worked with Mr. McDowell before. He doesn't mix business and pleasure. Besides, she's too . . . I don't know . . . too innocent for him. Not his type." He stopped. "We shouldn't be talking like this. They might hear. We might get fired. And anyway, it's wrong."

Genevieve had stopped in her tracks. She looked up at Lucas, embarrassment written across every feature. Suddenly, she grabbed his hand and pulled him silently back down the hall. Then, cheeks blazing, she took a deep breath. "How long do you think the repair and renovation of this place should take?" she asked loudly. Too loudly. Loud enough for the other men to hear. Clearly, she didn't want Thomas and Jorge to know what she had overheard.

"Everything has to be done in six weeks.

After that, we invite the world in, invite the tenants, and I leave town. Can you handle that?" he asked, playing along.

She took a deep, visible breath. "I can handle anything, Mr. McDowell." Her voice shook slightly, but it came out loud enough to carry.

They continued down the hall past the room where Thomas and Jorge were working. "I lied. I'd like to pretend that I know exactly what I'm doing, but I think it's clear that I'm learning. But I'll tell you this much, Lucas. Truthfully. Totally truthfully. I may not be able to handle everything yet, but I don't intend to slack off or slow down or disappoint you if I can help it. I intend to do my best at this job."

A nicer man would have assured her that that was enough. He had never been a nice man. "I intend to see that you do," he said. He hoped she would be able to produce the results that he needed. If everything worked out as planned, Genevieve would be his glowing gateway to the people he needed to reach.

But, by the end of the day, she wasn't glowing. Instead, she was wet, dirty and drooping. Strands of her bright hair had come loose from her tight ponytail and there was a scrape on her cheek. She looked as if she might drop to the ground at any minute.

"I'll take you home," he said. "Congratulations. You survived your first day." But he wondered whether she would be back for a second day or if she would choose to slink away, to decide that this was no life for a debutante.

Still, when he pulled up to her apartment, the sight of her crumbling and dangerous neighborhood reminded him that she had left debutante status behind. And he wasn't buying her declaration that she would never marry for money. Too long in a place like this and a woman — or a man — might do anything to get out. He knew about that kind of thing. Far too well, he thought with a grimace. Genevieve could get hurt. *She shouldn't be living here.*

The thought caught him by surprise. He never allowed his interactions with employees to get personal, but then this project *was* personal, the repayment of a long overdue debt. Finishing it would close a chapter in his life he never wanted to look back on again and tie up loose ends he couldn't control. Then, he could concentrate on a future he *could* control, one with zero emotional risks. Just the way he liked things.

"Thank you for the ride," Genevieve said,

reaching for the door, clearly uncomfortable. Probably not used to silent brooding bosses frowning at her.

"You don't . . . fit in a place like this," he said, stopping her and further surprising and angering himself.

To his amazement, she laughed, a light, bell-like sound. "I fit," she said. "We're all misfits here. I'm just not the norm."

Then she sprinted for her building, paying no attention to her surroundings, her purse flopping against her hip.

Darn it! But then, he supposed he shouldn't be surprised at her carelessness. A princess like her would have been used to leaving everything, including her security, to others.

Growling, he flung open his door and got out. "Genevieve," he said, his voice carrying.

She turned, those big eyes open wide, startled.

"Lock your door," he said. "I don't want to lose my project manager through carelessness," he felt compelled to add.

Genevieve blushed. She bit her lip. Was that a trace of resentment in her eyes? Intriguing. He hadn't seen that before.

"I have six locks," she told him, lifting her chin a tiny bit. There was just a trace of haughtiness, of the miffed debutante. "I . . . You don't really trust me, do you?"

He hesitated. "I hired you."

She nodded. "Because I'm a Patchett."

He wasn't going to deny it. Nor was he going to tell her he trusted her. He wasn't sure whether he did. The truth was, he had a suspicion that hiring her had been a mistake, for reasons that had nothing to do with the project, reasons he didn't even want to acknowledge. There was something about her that made him not trust *himself.* He had a terrible feeling that he knew what it was, too. It wasn't good.

But he had hired her. The only thing to do now was to muddle through this mess. Quickly. Soon enough Genevieve Patchett would just be another woman in the rear-view mirror of his consciousness. He was a pro at leaving bad situations — and problematic women — behind. If Genevieve was more problematic than most . . . well, he wouldn't let that happen. He'd tell her what she needed to know to do her job, oversee her progress from a distance and then he'd send her on her way with enough money to escape this place.

And both of them would walk away happy. End of story.

CHAPTER THREE

Genevieve lay in the dark, staring up at the ceiling but seeing instead the frown on Lucas's gorgeous face. Carefully, she went over what had taken place during the day. And cringed.

"You didn't even know how to sweep a floor, how to wash a wall." She groaned and placed her palms over her hot face. "The man must think that he's hired an idiot. He's probably cursing Teresa and me right now, probably already looking through his list of applicants for my replacement. I don't have any of the skills necessary, nothing that he wanted."

Worse than that, she had an annoying habit of blushing every time she looked at the man. With just one wordless glance, he had pointed out that her wet blouse was plastered to her body, and her reaction had been beyond embarrassment. Heat had slithered through her veins. Those steel-gray eyes had found her time and time again today, often wordlessly, and every time he had looked at her, she had felt like . . .

A woman when she should have felt like an employee. For two seconds she thought back to the days when she had appeared at all of her parents' balls and openings. What would Lucas have thought of her had he met her under such circumstances?

"Stop it right now, Gen," she ordered herself. She wasn't some silly romantic girl anymore. Besides, she most emphatically did not want a man, and Lucas certainly didn't want *her,* she thought, remembering Jorge's, Teresa's and Rita's words.

Besides, her very survival depended on her doing well at this job. And yet . . . in the back of her mind she heard her parents berating her for being awkward and for not being talented enough. She heard Barry mocking her for being such a sheltered, clueless princess. The thought that any day now Lucas might decide that she was incapable of doing her job . . .

Genevieve swallowed hard. Even the sound of yelling down the hall paled in comparison to her fears about what would happen if Lucas fired her. And it wasn't just about the money, either.

She sat up in bed and dashed away one

stray tear. "Don't cry, you idiot. *Do*. Learn. Prove to him that you're not afraid of anything." Even though she *was* desperately afraid. But she wasn't going to let Lucas know that.

"Odious, virile man," she whispered. "Other women have cried buckets over you, but I won't ever be one of them. I don't care what you think of me as long as I survive you and learn from you."

One thing she was sure of. When this was over, she would be more than glad to see the back of Lucas McDowell.

Lucas grunted as he flexed his arms, moving into his seventy-second push-up and trying to clear his thoughts. He was staying in the penthouse apartment of one of Chicago's most luxurious hotels and there was, of course, a gym available to him, but he had his own private regimen he followed. One hundred push-ups for starters. Every night. No exceptions. After the emotional chaos of his childhood, discipline had been his salvation. Nothing was going to change that.

But clearing his mind to concentrate on his task was proving difficult. After he'd left Genevieve at her apartment with her six locks, he'd searched the internet and easily located the crime statistics for that neighborhood. Theft was a given, domestic disputes the norm. He growled at that. He knew better than anyone that domestic dispute sounded much too mild for all the horrors that tag encompassed. But that had nothing to do with Genevieve.

"Not your problem or your business," he reminded himself. *Control the situation.* He repeated his mantra. *Don't let yourself get involved. Don't let the situation have power over you.* Because control was everything. It was the only thing that had kept him out of jail. It made life and success possible.

But in spite of his best efforts to stop thinking about Genevieve, when he tried to return to his task, he could still see the look in her eyes when she had told him that she had all those locks and asked him if he didn't trust her. Somehow he was sure she wouldn't appreciate him interfering in her life or suggesting that she might want to take her first paycheck and move.

It certainly wasn't the kind of thing he ever did or wanted to do. *Keep a distance. Never get too involved* was his motto.

And yet, Genevieve Patchett's naïveté, her dangerous situation, had kept him from completing a task he'd done every night for years. He was still stuck on push-up number seventy-two.

"Idiot. Get control of yourself. Stay out of this. Don't do something you'll regret." With a groan, he forced himself to complete the push-up and all the rest of them. Having withstood the onslaught of doubts and come out ahead, he went to bed. A soft bed. A safe bed. In an exclusive hotel in an exclusive neighborhood.

"And everything is perfectly fine," he mumbled. But in the middle of the night he woke from a dream in a cold sweat, his fears about why Genevieve was bothering him confirmed. Voices from a past he tried never to remember had pushed their way into his dreams. He'd heard his mother crying in the night. He'd felt his own failure, his inability to be what she wanted, and his own panic as she'd walked out the door, never to return. And after his father's death when he'd been left totally alone, there had been other mother figures, women who had tried to help him and recoiled in distress at his wounded animal anger. Some had been nice; most had merely wanted to use him to gild their reputations; one society princess had called him her "street child" until she had a baby of her own, a better, sweeter child, the kind she'd always wanted. In the end, he had spurned all of them. And then . . .

Lucas took a deep breath, knowing that there was no use trying to hold back the next part. Because the next was the worst, the most damning incident. Then, there had been Angie, an innocent girl who had been savagely beaten by her father just because she had been involved with a reckless troublemaker like Lucas. He'd known what her father was. He'd selfishly and arrogantly ignored it, urged her to defy her father and stay with him. And she had paid the price.

Anguish rushed over him at the memory of a young woman who had suffered at the fists of a full grown man, a woman who had never fully recovered, he had discovered only a few months ago.

Lucas cursed in the night. *There* was the connection. Angie. Because he'd known the danger that had existed for Angie and he'd ignored it, downplayed it. Just as he knew the danger for Genevieve.

Don't think about it. Don't get involved. Don't lose control. This is a different woman, a different situation, he told himself.

And the next day, he knew he was right. Genevieve and her situation were nothing like Angie. The Patchett princess got into his car wearing a pair of designer shoes, biscuit-colored slacks that would never survive the day and a gold silk blouse.

He studied her, and without thinking, he raised an eyebrow.

Genevieve stared back at him with just a tiny bit of defiance in her eyes. He was half-convinced that if he said anything about her clothes, she would sass him. But a second later, her cheeks turned pink, she looked away and he realized that he had been mistaken about the sass and the defiance. She was still just a little rich girl flailing around.

The fact that he couldn't keep his eyes off the V of her blouse or the way that sweet pink flush made her seem vulnerable and fragile and . . . enticing was irrelevant. Wasn't it?

Maybe. But once she was in the car, he was thankful that he had to keep his eyes off of her and on the road. It was a good reminder. *Always keep your eyes on the goal, the job, on whatever got you to where you wanted to go.* Goals were good. They kept a man from doing something he would regret later. And he would definitely regret doing anything . . . instinctive where Genevieve was concerned.

He glowered.

She was very silent. Maybe his glowering was scaring her.

Maybe he shouldn't have hired someone he could scare so easily. And yet . . .

"Did you survive yesterday all right?"

He knew the minute she turned to him. "Yes. Of course. You even told me that I survived before I went home."

"I know, but . . ." Damn, but he was bad at this sensitivity thing. "You were working hard. Muscles get sore. The next morning is sometimes tougher than the day before."

Her sudden chuckle was soft, whisperlike. "I may have been raised a privileged debutante and okay, maybe I *am* a little sore, but I'll get past it. Actually, it was rather nice . . . the feeling that I had actually used my own two hands to make a difference. So I'm fine, Lucas."

Okay, she was fine. And he was looking like an idiot. This was not the way he usually treated his employees. What was it about Genevieve Patchett that threw all of his thoughts out of whack?

He needed to get his thoughts back in line, restore discipline.

He would. He'd made his last mistake. Genevieve, he reminded himself, was no Angie. He didn't really have to worry about her. She was a pampered princess, and if she'd ever met him back in the day when he was a skinny, angry, dirty kid, she probably would have put her nose in the air and run the other way. Besides for the moment at least, she was his employee. He should be treating her as such. The job he had hired her for was too important, too meaningful for all this foolishness.

He turned his thoughts back to business, ignored the scent of her perfume. Why on earth was she wearing perfume when the smell of cleaning solution would overpower that delicate floral nonsense after a scant few minutes on the job?

"Before we get started this morning, I'd like to go over some paperwork with you, including your job description," he said, pulling up in front of Angie's House.

"All right. I'll look forward to it."

Those simple words, though soft, were delivered in a professional tone. And they did the trick. He and Genevieve were back to business. All that other stuff, her fragility, his annoying urge to protect, the way her perfume went straight to his senses and made him envision placing his lips on that enticing little pulse point in her throat . . . darn it, those were irrelevant. Thank goodness she knew how to speak "business style." As long as she kept that up, he could stop thinking of her as a woman. A good thing, because he needed to be her boss.

And nothing else.

Genevieve noticed the minute Lucas's demeanor changed. She had spent her whole life in the background, observing other people, so she was good at noting the little things that signaled a change in direction. Her parents had been volatile people, smiling at customers and sponsors one minute, screaming at their daughter for failing to do or be what they wanted the next. She had tried so hard to please them, but to no avail, and so she had learned to read the signs that a "berate Gen" attack was coming on. Even now her chest felt tight at the memory of those days.

It wasn't like that with Lucas. Nothing volatile, no yelling, even though she sensed that under the right circumstances, he could be very dangerous. He was, as Teresa had told her, strong and silent. Still, she noticed the subtle change when he moved from frustrated concern about her having overdone things the day before into total businessman mode.

And, she told herself, it was a relief to have all that intense concern and attention turned away from her. Wasn't it?

Yes, she thought, because Lucas was too overwhelming as it was. Having him paying attention to her, and worse, she admitted, *liking* the attention, would lead her down the "you're going to regret this later" road. So, she forced herself to concentrate on the task at hand.

"You've had a chance to spend a day in the house and get the lay of the land. Now let's discuss what we can do with the rooms and how we can best utilize the space that we have."

This was new territory for Gen. Her parents had a massive home, but they traveled so much that, beyond the bedrooms and studios, most of the rooms were seldom used. They were filled with art, were cleaned by the staff, but there didn't seem to be any purpose to them.

"You'll be a better judge of what women need than I do. What do you think?" Lucas asked as they stared at a large sunny room.

Think, Gen, think. So far you've done nothing to justify Lucas's hiring you other than having a recognizable name. "I think . . . this would be a good place for the women to gather, to talk, to share secrets," she said, struggling for a good response, remembering her own "travel here and there" lifestyle that had precluded building the kind of friendships other girls had. "I'd — I think I'd paint it a soft color, maybe add some comfortable couches and possibly put in lots of big floor pillows. And we could . . . yes, we could add a table where they could work on crafts or sit and share tea or coffee," she said, picking up steam and forgetting that she didn't really know what she was talking about. She had never had any real contact with poor women who had truly suffered. But she knew what *she* would like. Maybe those women would like some of the same things.

"That wall would be perfect for a bank of bookshelves. And we could also add a hideaway television or hang one on the wall, so they could watch movies together. If it were my house, that is," she said, finally remembering that she was on virgin ground here as she hesitantly turned to Lucas. He had a slightly amused expression on that too handsome face.

Uh-oh, she had gone overboard, hadn't she? Her parents, despite being artists, had been practical people and they had always told her that she was far too much of a dreamer. That's why they had wanted her to marry Barry, a man of numbers, one who would overshadow the nonsensical daydreamer part of her and keep her out of trouble.

Hmm, that was a plan that had failed

miserably, but that didn't mean they hadn't been right about the daydreaming. Spending her time making up castles in the air hadn't prepared her for the real world and her current lifestyle at all.

"Those things you mentioned, is that what you did with *your* girlfriends?" Lucas asked.

"It's what I think the women who'll live here *might* want to do," she said, trying not to sound too defensive. She was most definitely *not* going to tell Lucas how few friends she'd had. She already looked pathetic enough as it was.

"Then it sounds like a very good idea," he said. "Excellent, in fact."

At the words of praise a glow began deep inside Genevieve. No one had ever applauded her ideas before.

Well, don't make too much of it. Teresa said that Lucas was a good boss. He probably praises everyone's ideas.

"Where to next?" she asked.

"Well, after that, I don't think there's any need to do a play-by-play of each room. You seem to have the right idea. Instead, let's move on to the big-picture plan. Come on. I had Jorge set up a control room last night."

"A control room?"

"Yes. Once we get you set up and comfortable, I'll return to my hotel where I have a bank of offices to oversee McDowell Sporting Goods and the other projects I'm involved in. I'll drop in to check on the progress of Angie's House and for public events, but you'll be spearheading things, so you'll need an office. It's just at the top of the stairs."

Genevieve followed him into a room that had been totally empty yesterday. Now it was filled with the latest technology, furniture, a bookcase filled with reference materials on the city, a cabinet full of supplies and a state-of-the-art sound system. There were pictures on the wall, curtains at the windows, a fresh paint smell and new carpeting.

Blinking, she shook her head. "All this for a job that will end in a few weeks?"

He shrugged. "All my jobs end in a few weeks."

Which she supposed she already knew. Lucas was renowned for coming to a town, getting a buzz going, setting up a new store and then moving on. Surely he must have one place he called home, but if so, Teresa had said, he didn't share that info. It was a good thing to remember. The man was both temporary and a mystery. And she'd had enough of secretive activities and men who left you empty-handed.

"Thank you for being so thorough," she said. "I'm sure I'll find everything I need here." If only she knew exactly what she needed to do.

"Here's what you'll be doing," Lucas said, as if he'd read her mind. He came up beside her. And for some reason she didn't want to examine, her heart began to pound. He was much taller than her with broad shoulders and he exuded virility the way desert sand exuded heat waves. Standing this close, she felt small, feminine, as if her whole body was waiting for something to happen.

Then he reached around her and picked up a stack of papers. His arm brushed hers.

Genevieve's breath stalled in her throat. She hoped he hadn't noticed how aware of him she was. It would be a good idea for her to step away. But would a strong, sensible, seasoned project manager do that just because a good-looking man was standing beside her? Of course not. With a great effort, she modulated her breathing. In. Out. *Show no emotion. Try to look professional, Gen.*

Thankfully, Lucas stepped aside quickly. He held the papers out to her. "Here's the agenda, all that has to be accomplished during the next few weeks. I want you to avail yourself of whatever resources you need and if you need additional personnel let me know. You will, of course, have an expense account. Also, for the next few days, until you get acclimated, I'll drop in from time to time and you can also update me on the way to and from work. Thereafter, I'll provide you with a driver and we'll meet at scheduled times for updates just as I do with my other employees and my other business. I'll be available for any public events you set up. So . . . are there any questions or concerns? Things you want to talk about?"

Gen looked down at the list. It was long. She was to oversee Thomas and Jorge in the renovation and decoration of the house itself, and introduce herself and the project to the neighbors, possibly by hosting a neighborhood gathering. She was expected to locate sponsors for the women and donors for future projects, contact charities for prospective candidates to live at Angie's House, establish links between local community colleges for classes and training sessions for the women, contact possible employers for those women who needed work, arrange for the open house, interview candidates and hire a director. In several places, he had noted that she could rely on him and on her own social contacts to smooth the way and drum up interest.

Did she have concerns? She had them in spades, although pulsating fears that turned her legs to jelly might be a better way to phrase it. This was beyond anything she had ever done for her parents and so much of it seemed to rely on using her family name. Genevieve wanted to close her eyes, to try and explain to Lucas just how little influence she had. Her parents had been the movers and shakers, while she had been an insignificant shadow in the background. And after Barry had spread all those ugly, damning and humiliating lies about her, no one was ever in this lifetime going to care what she had to say. About anything. But if she told Lucas that . . .

"I have to be honest, Lucas. I don't think my name is going to have much influence. My parents were the 'capital *P*' Patchetts. That's not me."

He studied her, looking down at her shoes. "Genevieve, look at yourself. Look at that little patrician nose of yours, that perfect posture and those long, slender artist's fingers. Listen to the way you enunciate your words. You may be living in less elegant surroundings right now, but you're still a Patchett." With that, he reached out and touched the silk of her blouse. His finger didn't even make contact with her skin, but she felt as if it did. An awareness of him thrummed through her, sending warmth down her body in a rush. "You're still a princess."

With some effort, she raised her chin. "I'm sorry if I misled you, but I was never a princess."

"I see. So . . . you don't think you can do this?"

Genevieve swallowed hard. "I just don't think that anyone who was wild about my parents is going to transfer that esteem to me."

"No? Do me a favor. Do that thing you did yesterday when you suggested that I didn't trust you. Give me that look of defiance. Raise your chin just a touch."

Flustered, Genevieve tried to do as he asked, but she was too self-conscious. And she wasn't angry at him.

Lucas frowned. "You can do better than that. You *know* what I need from you. But I'm going to have to let you go if you can't do this job the way it needs to be done. I won't want to, but I need someone who can produce and produce quickly. If you can't do that, then I'm afraid you're gone." His voice dropped lower, the last words barely a whisper, but the steel in his tone was unmistakable. He would be ruthless if need be.

And like that, the desperation of her situation kicked in. Anger that she was failing and that yet another person was dismissing her overshadowed all of her fears. This time she didn't just lift her chin. She threw her shoulders back the way she had been taught by a long-ago posture coach and she raised her head in what could only be called a regal gesture. "I won't be gone," she said and though her voice barely carried from her mouth to his ears, there was determination in her tone. "Don't fire me," she said. "Just . . . don't."

He stared at her with those fierce, dark, bird-of-prey eyes of his and she managed not to flinch. But when he still hadn't said anything, she finally dropped her gaze. "Please don't," she said.

A low curse issued from his lips. "I hired you for a very good reason. I'm counting on you to be what I need you to be," he said. "And I'm not firing you." She waited for the word *yet,* but it didn't come. That didn't mean that he wasn't thinking it. It was do-or-die time for her. She might not know what she was doing, but that couldn't matter. She was going to do something.

CHAPTER FOUR

The woman was a danger to his composure. Lucas hated that. He had almost told her that she could have the job no matter what she did or didn't do. And what kind of a mess would that turn out to be? Had he forgotten how important this project was or the promises he had made just a few months ago? To a woman he had wronged and never righted the wrong. To a woman . . . no — to *many* women whose anguished eyes still haunted him.

No. He would never forget. He would go to his grave trying to fulfill those promises. And he would not allow anything to stand in the way of completing Angie's House on time.

Still, he could surely afford a few days to give Genevieve a chance to find her bearings. His controlling ways seemed to be detrimental to her composure and confidence. Maybe if he stayed away from her, she'd have a better chance of success.

"Sure, put it that way, McDowell," he muttered. The truth was that he just needed to stay far enough away from her to regain *his* composure. There was just something about Genevieve with her prim, pouty little mouth, her hair that was pulled back so hard that it had to hurt and her slender little body and delicate, haughty chin that made him want to . . .

Cover that mouth with his own, slide his hands into that hair and send the pins flying, mold that sweet, perfect body to his.

And that was the real reason he was staying away. Maybe that flare-up with Rita and the fact that he had spent most of the past six months alone was just making him crazy for any woman. No matter. He was going to give Genevieve some room to run.

So, he did his best to stay away, concentrate on his legitimate business and not think about Genevieve at all beyond the sphere of work.

Except he still drove her to and from Angie's House and stopped in for a progress report every single day.

That kept her in his sights, in his thoughts. He hated that. Staying with one woman, letting any woman slip behind his defenses, wasn't allowed. He had good reasons for that. This was a nonnegotiable item.

As for Genevieve and her progress, at first she was tentative in her reports. "I was thinking that it might be nice for each woman to be able to have some say in what her room, her personal retreat, will be like. So I thought perhaps . . . maybe . . . we should make each bedroom look finished but still leave room for more decorating after the women move in. They can perhaps . . . possibly . . . accessorize and make the rooms their own."

Lucas wasn't a man who smiled much, but he couldn't hold back a trace of a smile now. "That's a great idea, Genevieve. No 'maybe' or 'perhaps' or 'possibly' about it," he teased.

"Oh." Her lips parted as if he'd caught her by surprise. Her green eyes opened wide, all bright and sparkly. She looked as if he had handed her the keys to a treasure. She was beautiful. Radiant. He wanted to move closer.

It was a terrible idea, but he couldn't seem to stop himself. He took her hand, her incredibly soft hand with its long, slender fingers, and her palm with its sweet center just meant for a man's lips. As if that involuntary thought was controlling his actions, he raised her hand, his mouth only inches away from all that soft skin.

Stop, he warned himself.

She looked taken aback. He hadn't spoken that *stop* out loud, had he? Or maybe it was the near kiss that had upset her. Either way . . .

"It's a great idea," he said again, releasing her. "Keep up the good work." And then he made some stupid excuse and rushed away. He intended to give her several days free and clear of his company. At least as much as possible. He incorporated their daily reports into their drive time. He kept things businesslike, dry. Things should have been totally impersonal as they always were with his employees.

And yet they never were. As they drove down the mean streets, she seemed to notice everything and everyone and her heart bled for all of them. "Look at that poor man," she said one day, pointing out a man who appeared to be begging for money not for himself but for the sick boy beside him, a boy who was playing kick ball when Lucas drove by the next day. She exclaimed about the woman with a baby carriage struggling over the bumpy parts of the street. Or a stray puppy. Or a man trying to sell newspapers that no one seemed to want to buy.

Genuine tragedy or scam, Genevieve ached for all of them. He had a bad feeling that sooner or later someone would take advantage of her soft heart.

Stop thinking about her, he ordered himself. She wouldn't want his advice or want to hear of his concern. *I have six locks,* she had said, clearly disgusted by him even asking. He needed to just forget about her situation.

She wasn't his concern, was she? Except . . . she was — damn her — another woman in peril. Another Angie. It almost seemed as if fate were mocking him by sending him someone like Genevieve just when he was trying to effect a change that would enable him to forever be free of her kind of woman. A woman in trouble, one whose situation was beyond his control when control was what he had always needed most, what he couldn't survive without.

So, he cursed fate. He tried to ignore Genevieve's situation and just get on with the project as quickly as possible.

Until the night when there was another robbery in her neighborhood.

And there it was. Again. His past breathing down his neck. Hot. Frightening. Careening out of control. No way to control the situation at all. He remembered Angie, who had lived in fear her whole life. Angie, whose life had been changed forever because of two men who should have protected her but who hurt and failed her and, ultimately, destroyed her.

Damn it, he had been one of those men and he could *not* survive hurting another woman like that or standing by and letting one get hurt when he had the means to stop it. Because he knew — all too well — that it was only a matter of time before someone noticed that a delicate flower like Genevieve was living smack in the middle of a "no holds barred, no crime left uncommitted" zone.

She would end up being hurt because he had left her there.

Because you have absolutely no right to interfere. She told you earlier in every way possible that she wants to fight clear of that place herself. And when that happened, she would no doubt return to the glassed-off world of the privileged, where rough men like him didn't belong. That was a good thing.

Still, Lucas didn't do a single push-up that night. His control that he had always relied on failed him.

Because damn it, he knew the streets like he knew his own thoughts. Six locks or eight locks or even ten locks wouldn't matter if the bad guys wanted in.

One good look at Genevieve and they would want in.

Lucas swore. He waited for the morning. And then he went to Angie's House.

Surely, if he did this right, he could get Genevieve out of his mind. Then he could go back to moving on with his life. And Genevieve could return to being . . . someone who didn't matter to him at all beyond this project.

Thank goodness.

"So get on with it, McDowell. Make a deal with the woman. Get her out of your thoughts. Now. Today."

Genevieve looked around the small den, which was substantially cleaner than when she had entered it at the beginning of the day. Then she looked down at herself. Okay, the delicate piping around the edge of the neckline of her top was slightly damp, there were a few dust smudges here and there, but unlike some of the other outfits she'd been wearing, this one might live to see another day.

An inordinate sense of accomplishment brought a smile to her face. "I did it," she said to no one in particular.

"Did what?" Lucas's unmistakable deep

91

voice came from the doorway, and Gen whirled to find him studying her intently.

Automatically some major fluttering began in her stomach. She frowned at her own foolish reaction and squelched it until only a few tiny flutters remained.

"I . . ." She held out her hand. "It's dumb."

He waited.

"I cleaned an entire room by myself. I mean, it's not perfect." Because now that he was here, she was noticing that she had missed some dust on the windowsill and there were still a few cobwebs here and there and . . .

"It's good," he said.

Which might have seemed like faint praise to most people, but to a woman used to no praise? His words were truthful. Not over-blown. He hadn't said "great," which she would have known was a lie. He had said "good" . . . which was the precise word to describe what she'd done.

"I . . ."

"Say thank you, Genevieve," he suggested.

"Yes. Thank you. Did you need something? Is there something I need to do?"

He came into the room then. "Actually, there is. Have Thomas and Jorge gone home?"

She nodded. "Ten minutes ago."

"Good. We need to talk."

Uh-oh, the fact that he wanted her out of earshot of anyone else . . .

"Is there something I've done wrong?"

"No. It's simply that I've decided that it would be a good idea if you stayed here instead of your apartment."

"Here?" Away from that rat hole where she'd been living? Away from Mrs. Dohenny's shrieks and accusations about the remaining few dollars she still owed? A sudden whoosh of relief rushed in. And then . . . it rushed out again. There was something calculating in Lucas's expression and tone. Something wasn't quite right.

Perhaps what wasn't right was the fact that she had been so excited she hadn't yet asked the obvious question. "Why?"

He shrugged. "It's more convenient here, for one thing. Having you here will save time, speed up the process. Are you telling me that you'd rather stay where you are than live here?"

No. No. No. She just suddenly felt that there was something she was missing. Just as she had with Barry. And she felt as if a man was once again making personal decisions for her when the last time that had happened she had ended up with her self-esteem wrecked and her world in tatters.

"Mr. McDowell," she began, trying to create some distance. It didn't work. He raised that lofty, dark eyebrow. "Lucas," she amended. "I know my apartment might be a bit . . . distasteful. And it's probably a nuisance having to pick me up and bring me home, but I can work around that. You don't have to drive me. Even with the construction, there's another bus stop only a mile and a half away. I can walk from there."

"I'm not worried about driving into your neighborhood, Genevieve. I lived in places like that long-term and I know what it's like. It's no place for a princess."

She raised her chin. "I told you, I'm not a princess. Or even a debutante anymore. What I am is a grown woman, Lucas." She wanted to add that she was a *strong* woman, but that would be a lie. She wasn't there yet. Not nearly. Right now she was awkward, with no street sense, and she was making a lot of mistakes. But she wanted to be strong. And much as she wanted out of her apartment, letting a man make that choice for her, even a man she needed to please to keep her job . . . well, she had to try to have some say in this.

"You're a woman, an adult," Lucas admit-

ted, his voice dark and deep, sending shiv-
ers through her. "But if someone bigger,
stronger tried to take everything you own,
you couldn't prevent that from happening."

Her courage and confidence were failing
her. She wasn't used to arguing. She'd never
been good at it; her parents had always won
every disagreement. Furthermore, Lucas
was her boss. Arguing with him felt really
wrong, but she just couldn't seem to stop
thinking about how Barry had bullied her
and betrayed her. She couldn't seem to stop
trying to assert herself. "You don't know
that I couldn't defend myself. I could have
had kickboxing lessons."

He tilted his head. "Have you?"

Darn her need for honesty! "No."

At least he didn't look triumphant the way
Barry would have when he had won a point.

"Genevieve," he said, looking suddenly
tired and exasperated. He rubbed his palm
over the back of his neck. "Why does this
mean so much to you?"

She looked down. "I can't afford to move
here. I still owe a little money to Mrs.
Dohenny, my landlady."

"I'll pay it."

"No! No! I haven't earned that much yet.
And —"

"And . . . ?"

She looked up then, daring to stare directly into those mesmerizing see-all gray eyes. "I know this sounds foolish." And she was so tired of being thought foolish or inconsequential. Everyone she'd ever loved had thought of her that way. "The thing is . . . I'm penniless because my fiancé, who happened to be my financial advisor, tricked me out of my money. When that happened, I was humiliated, angry and clueless about how to go on, because all my life I'd let other people make my decisions.

"That was when I realized just how precious and important and empowering independence really is. So, I really need to make my own way in the world. No charity involved. No letting other people make my decisions. Of course, I understand that you have the right to control anything regarding my work, but please. This is where I live. It's not work."

He studied her for a minute, frowning.

"I apologize if I've made you angry," she began, which seemed to make him *really* angry. He cut her off with a sudden slashing of his hand.

"If you want to be truly independent, you should speak your mind. No apologies. No letting me push you around when I've overstepped the boundaries of our work relationship."

She bit her lip.

"Just as you did a moment ago," he emphasized.

"All right. Then we can stop talking about my apartment? And I'll take the bus from now on."

Lucas opened his mouth to speak but the doorbell rang at that moment. He tilted his head and started to move toward the door at the same time as she did.

Genevieve stopped. So did Lucas. Then he waved her through. "My apologies. You're the project manager, and Angie's House and any visitors here are in your hands. We'll continue this discussion later."

Which meant that she hadn't won. Yet.

Stubborn, overbearing, infuriating man. No wonder women fell all over themselves trying to attract his attention. It must be the prospect of attaining the unattainable.

Thank goodness she wasn't that susceptible.

Lucas watched Genevieve walk away, knowing he was handling this situation all wrong.

The truth was that Genevieve tied him up in frustrated knots. He admired her for sticking to her guns, but he needed to have her settled, clear of his conscience and out of his private thoughts. If she was here, safe, he wouldn't have to think about her at all beyond the job. He would have compartmentalized her situation, controlled the danger zones, the loose ends, the tough, emotional stuff that had once made his life a nightmare. Plus, if she truly wanted to be empowered . . .

His thoughts were interrupted by Genevieve appearing in the doorway.

"That was a delivery of paint primer," she told him with a frown.

"Something wrong with the order?"

She shook her head. "No, but up until now you and I have only *spoken* about what's happening at Angie's House. Here I was all set to show my stuff and prove that I could handle any situation, and all I had to do was tell him where to put everything. Nothing even remotely challenging about that."

Lucas couldn't help smiling just a little. "Don't worry. You'll face plenty of challenges before we're through. There are always setbacks and glitches. I suppose you're looking forward to those."

She looked at him suspiciously. "Is this a trick question?"

He chuckled. "No, no tricks, but if it's empowerment you're after . . ."

"It is."

"Then come stay here." Like a dog that couldn't ignore the bone, he came back to the topic that was keeping thoughts of Genevieve simmering in his conscience.

"That's not empowerment. It's giving in."

A trickle of admiration at her tenacity slid through Lucas. He knew Gen didn't like conflict, but she was making a stand. Too bad her stand conflicted with his. And with a cold, hard truth.

"It's not giving in," he said. "Think about this. A lot of the women who'll come to live at Angie's House know all about neighborhoods like yours because they've been there, they're trapped there. If they see you as someone who's lived in that world, kicked free and survived to grow stronger . . . that's inspirational and empowering. It makes you a role model."

She stood there, staring at him, her eyes wary. "It feels exactly like quitting."

"It's not. Gen, a good portion of the residents where I used to live stayed there because they were powerless to get away or change their circumstances. I was like that. Getting out empowered me and changed my life. It meant that I was taking control of the situation."

Lucas didn't miss the war taking place in

99

Genevieve's eyes. She wanted to take up his offer, but taking what she saw as the easy way out didn't fit with her new life's plan to be a strong woman. He was losing her.

As he'd lost others.

No. No. Strike that thought. Focus on the now, on taking charge, making things right. So, he fought his instincts, fought the urge to put his fist through something. In the past he would have done just that. But not now. Now he was all about control. Control was survival.

So he couldn't stop. Not until he had made sure Genevieve was safe and until he'd restored the "no personal interest" parameters of their relationship and kicked free of his fascination with her. It was the only way he could continue to function with her, given his past. Given what he'd learned about Angie.

He ached to turn back time and save Angie, but he couldn't. The only one he could save today was Genevieve. But he didn't want to break her spirit. He couldn't let the cost be too high.

Lucas cleared his throat, cleared his mind, focused on the key elements, on the truth. He knew how much she valued the truth.

"Genevieve, I won't deny that I'm worried about you living in such a dangerous place, mostly because I know all about predators and the damage they do." He glanced away. That was enough of that. She didn't need to know more.

"But as I said, think about the good you could do if you became the first resident of Angie's House. Your experiences these past few months would help you understand what these women, the future residents, have dealt with for years. The simple act of standing in their shoes could be very useful in your job." His voice trailed off. There was nothing more that he could say. If she didn't want to move here, if his arguments hadn't convinced her, he couldn't — and wouldn't — try to force her.

For several seconds Genevieve said nothing. She closed her eyes. When she opened them again, she was frowning. "You're used to controlling your empire, aren't you?"

Her voice sounded wistful, but she quickly rushed on. "I didn't mean that quite the way it sounded."

She stood there looking beaten. For a moment, Lucas wanted to take back everything he'd said even though all of it was true.

But he didn't. He waited, hoping for a positive outcome. Eventually, she took a deep, visible breath and pushed her shoulders back in that way he'd seen her do when she was facing adversity. She plastered on a resigned smile. A small smile. "So, you think moving here will help me do my job better. Are you sure you're not just giving me an easy way out?"

He couldn't help himself then. He dropped his head and groaned. Then he laughed. "Gen, do you call the conversation we just had taking the easy way out?"

When he looked up, she was smiling. "I guess it *was* pretty uncomfortable. But let me ask you this. Why do you care where I live?"

"Why does it matter where you live?" Man, there was the tough question. Lucas wondered if he even understood all the reasons why. And he had no intention of examining his motives too closely. There certainly wasn't a chance in hell that he would tell Genevieve about waking up in the night. Or about Angie or any of the rest.

Letting her know that he'd lived in poverty? That was common knowledge. The fact that he had pulled himself out of the gutter and become a success was part of what engendered respect among his peers and the public. But sharing more? No. He never let anyone in on the more intimate details of his life, especially those from his past.

"Beyond the reasons I've already given you," he said. "Let's just say that I can't have my employees getting hurt. And think how bad it would look for Angie's House if anyone thought that I paid my project manager so poorly that she had to live in a place where she needed six locks on her door." He finished with a smile, trying to somehow turn this into something light and teasing. Because now he knew how much she longed for independence and pride, a need he understood all too well.

Genevieve tilted her head. "You're very good at getting your way, aren't you?"

Her voice was wistful. He felt as if he'd just manhandled a defenseless kitten. "I don't like unpredictable situations, especially when they pertain to work," he admitted.

"And this *is* work." Her tone was questioning.

"Yes." He wouldn't let it be anything else.

"You'll let me pay rent."

"No." Not when he was practically forcing her into this transition. Not when he needed her to make this change as much as she needed it.

But he could see she was going to object. "It's work, remember?" he said. "Part of your job."

She still didn't look totally convinced, but finally she nodded. "Well, then. All right, Lucas. I'll live in Angie's House and I'll try to make use of the extra hours I'll be there to get more done."

Lucas scowled at that. He controlled things but he didn't overwork his employees. "Overtime isn't necessary."

Genevieve had a trapped look in her eyes. Her slender body trembled and she licked her lips nervously. Finally, she closed her eyes, then looked to the side, lifting her chin a bit imperiously. "I would like to ask you to reconsider that point at least. If I'm your project manager and my staying here is to set the reputation of Angie's House and bring attention to it, then I should have some say in how things proceed, shouldn't I? The goal of Angie's House is to reenergize the spirit of the women who live here, you told me. So, as the first inhabitant . . . I would very much like to either pay rent or work overtime in order to feel that I am truly contributing and so that my spirit will be reenergized."

She never raised her voice, but it was clear that if he said no, she would feel as if he didn't value her service. And after the heavy-handed method he had used to get her to agree to this change . . .

Lucas swore beneath his breath. Okay, she had him over a barrel. He could push the issue, but . . . she was clearly a woman who had been misused, whose ego had been trampled. And he had sworn he'd never damage a fragile female again. It was another reason why he only dated women like Rita, women who were just as cold and calculating as he was.

Genevieve was nothing like Rita. She wasn't cold enough, hard enough or experienced enough. In fact, he should never have hired her, but . . . letting her go would certainly damage her. She'd be out on the streets with nowhere to go. Now that he fully understood that . . .

"A little overtime would be all right," he conceded. Because in the end he had gotten what he wanted, hadn't he? She would be safe. That meant he wouldn't have to think about her anymore. From that moment on, the two of them would only be about the job.

But hours later he realized that moving her hadn't totally solved the Genevieve problem. Vulnerable green eyes crept into his thoughts. He knew why, too. He owned Angie's House. And even though he was staying in a high-rent hotel all the way across town, the truth was that Genevieve was now living, breathing and sleeping beneath his roof.

Right now she was probably lying in bed.

Lucas groaned. He tried not to think about Genevieve's beautiful copper-colored hair spread out across a pillow or those long bare legs. . . .

"Stop it. Don't go there. Just . . . speed this up. Let's get this done — finished — so you can walk away as you always do," he whispered. It was a good plan. Two months from now, Genevieve Patchett would no doubt be back making the debutante rounds, and he would be far away. She would barely be a blip in his memory base.

Which was . . . excellent, because if this heat and temptation kept building, he would be kissing Genevieve's pretty pink lips any day now.

And that would be the worst kind of mistake.

But it wasn't going to happen. Order had been restored to his life. His solitary journey could continue.

He could finally get Genevieve out of his thoughts, couldn't he?

CHAPTER FIVE

The day after Genevieve moved in, she tried to throw herself into work, opting to paint one of the bedrooms herself, even though Thomas and Jorge were better painters. She needed activity. Not just planning. She needed to immerse herself in something purely physical, so that she wouldn't have time to think. Because the truth was that already she was having trouble adapting to living in Angie's House.

She knew why, too. This place was very nice. It was quiet and safe and even a bit lovely now that the decorating was beginning to take shape. But she just couldn't seem to forget that Lucas owned this house. Living here, eating and sleeping and dreaming here . . . it all felt too physical, and she'd already discovered that she was very susceptible to Lucas's touch. She couldn't be thinking about him all the time or risk getting close to him.

Which was a ridiculous thing to worry about. He wasn't about to let an employee get close. In truth, she knew very little about the man. She knew that he was rich, she'd searched around online and discovered that he had other philanthropic projects he was involved in besides this one. He provided free sporting goods to inner-city schools, he sponsored summer camps for poor children. What she didn't know about him was anything . . . personal.

Except that for some reason he had decided to do more than give money to charity this time. He was personally involved in this charitable venture. Sometimes when he spoke about women who had terrible, frightening lives, a fleeting look of something, maybe anguish, came into his eyes. She'd seen it but she didn't understand it at all.

Then, too, this place was called Angie's House. Had there been an Angie or was it just a convenient moniker? And if there had been an Angie, had he been in love with her? Had he —

"Genevieve?" Lucas's deep voice sounded behind her.

Genevieve jumped. She dropped the paintbrush onto the drop cloth, splattering blue paint, then rushed to pick it up, trying to hide her blush and her embarrassment.

"I'm sorry," Lucas said. "I startled you. I should have made more noise or —"

Suddenly, he stopped talking and Genevieve looked up to see what had interrupted his speech. He was looking at the walls, which were . . .

A mess. A series of loops and sloppy brushstrokes. Obviously, she had taken her erratic thoughts about Lucas and translated them to her work. Embarrassment rushed through her. And Lucas was shaking his head.

"Genevieve, why are you painting?" he asked. "I thought we agreed that you had completed your hands-on tasks."

They had. "I —" His frown sent her words stumbling. She looked at the walls that appeared to have been painted by a child. All of this would have to be redone. More paint. More work. More time wasted when she knew he was already on a tight deadline. The other day when he'd been there he'd received a phone call regarding the job in France. They needed him there soon, possibly sooner than originally planned. If he'd hired someone more experienced than she was . . . maybe he *would* hire someone like that and let her go. She hadn't made nearly enough progress. "Lucas, I know I haven't lived up to expectations yet. But I will. I promise."

To her surprise she wanted to add, *Please don't send me away,* but that was too personal. It sounded too much like she wanted to stay here to be with *him.* Thank goodness her voice was shaking too much and her sense of self-preservation stopped her. Why was she even thinking such a crazy thought, anyway? Most likely because Lucas had voiced concern about her safety. That must be all it was, because certainly he was nothing to her. She didn't want to feel anything for him.

But she couldn't stop herself from looking up at him. And what she saw there wasn't anger, but something that looked a lot more like sadness, a hint of pain. It flickered in his eyes and then it was gone.

Heaven help her, but she wanted to move close to him and touch him, to apologize again for not being what he had expected. She knew this project was important to him. She hated the fact that she was messing things up.

And the fact that she wanted to help him, to touch him?

It totally petrified her. It was like looking over the rim of the Grand Canyon and feeling your feet slipping. She seriously needed to step away from the edge Lucas represented.

Lucas looked at the loopy, layered paint on the wall. When he had come across Genevieve she had been painting away, clearly involved in her thoughts instead of her work and going at the wall with vigor.

He wondered if that Barry guy, that ex-fiancé who had cleaned out her accounts, had tried to contact her again. Was that what had her so distressed?

Lucas felt a growl coming on. Why was he even thinking such thoughts when Genevieve's personal life was none of his business?

Darn right, but . . . she *was* distressed and right now she was on his property, in his employ, living under his roof. That made her . . . his.

No! It didn't. It simply made him partly responsible for her, especially since he clearly had her scared to death that he was going to let her go.

Grr. Damn him for being an unfeeling jerk. Lucas shook his head. "I'm not going to fire you, Gen. Stop that. I'm sorry I ever even mentioned that possibility." While having her here was proving to be more complicated than he had hoped, she was working hard, she was trying, she had met him halfway on moving here when she hadn't wanted to and she had some good ideas on how to dress up this place. And there was one more reason he didn't intend to fire her. He just didn't want to hurt her.

Hadn't he already done that? Because the fact that she was scared and afraid of losing her job was a kind of hurt, wasn't it?

When he'd mentioned letting her go, it hadn't really been because of what she'd done or not done, but because of how she affected him. She awakened hard-to-control desire in him. His problem, not hers. Threatening her with termination had been a purely selfish, defensive move. An ugly move. But then, he'd done ugly, selfish things before. And Angie, at least, was still paying the price.

Lucas tensed again as the memories of all the people he'd hurt and who had hurt him threatened to descend. *Control the situation,* he told himself.

"Genevieve, don't worry about the wall. It's just paint. Not life or death. It's fixable." When so many things in life weren't fixable. Like a woman who had been scarred because the person she most trusted and cared about had failed to protect her.

"Lucas?"

He looked down at Genevieve. Those big green eyes were worried. "You don't have to be gentle with me just because I'm inexperienced and still learning the basics. I can tell that you're angry."

"I'm not angry at *you*."

To his surprise she crossed her arms and gave him an incredulous look. "You're positively glowering. Lucas, I told you I'm not a child. Just look at this mess. It wasn't incompetence but inattentiveness and I won't make that mistake again. Here, I'll show you. I'm going to totally fix it. Right now." She reached for the paintbrush.

That was when he noticed the cut on her hand. And was it his imagination or was she thinner than before? Were those circles beneath her pretty eyes? Was she losing sleep, trying to get this job done for him, to finish up that long list he'd given her in a too-short time frame while he'd failed to notice because he was trying to keep his distance from her?

A rough word escaped his lips. Reaching out, he gently grasped her hand, resting it on his much larger palm as he examined it closely. There were scrapes, a long, thin cut. "You're hurt," he said, his voice harsh.

"No, I — I'm fine. I just . . . snagged it on the paint-can opener. I was rushing, trying to do things too fast. Not anything major. It's fine." But her fingers trembled against his. Her entire body was trembling.

"Gen, you're not fine. You're pushing yourself too hard. I caused this, didn't I? With my talk of how important it was to get in there and do the tough stuff and that stupid comment I made about letting you go . . . I — damn, you'd think a man like me would have already learned how easy it is to hurt someone, wouldn't you? I'm sorry for letting it come to this."

"No, Lucas. Really. Please don't apologize. Don't think I'm fragile or that I have to be protected or treated with some sort of deference because I lack experience. I don't want that."

She had scrambled closer. He still held her hand and now she placed her other hand on his chest. To stop him. To shut him up. He felt her touch right down to his core.

"I know," he said with the smallest of smiles. "You're one tough lady. You're independent," he managed to say. "But, Gen, you're trembling. Is it because you thought that I might fire you? I'm sorry if I scared you."

"No. I'm okay. If you said I could stay, then I trust that you meant it."

"You trust me." *Don't trust me,* he wanted

to say. How many women had trusted him and regretted it when he'd failed them?

"Yes. And I'm past that weakness I had a moment ago. I'm embarrassed about it and I'm better now. I'm strong."

And as she looked up at him with those big green eyes, trying so hard to show him how strong she was . . . she was so very close, so soft, so determined, so earnest . . .

"You're strong. I'm glad," he said, covering her hand on his chest with his palm. The movement brought her closer and sent her fingers sliding against his skin. The sensation . . . he thought his heart might just pound its way out of his body. He looked at Genevieve, at those eyes, those soft pouting lips he coveted and . . .

"I'm strong, too, Genevieve, but I'm afraid I'm just not strong enough to resist this," he said, and with one tug he pulled her into his arms. His mouth covered hers and finally, finally he got to taste her. She tasted of fresh peaches and intriguing woman and something else, something he couldn't describe. But he liked it. He wanted it. He kissed her again, nearly devoured her as he began to lose control.

Her arm came around his waist. Her head tilted back. She returned his kiss, pleasing him. Very much. A tiny moan escaped her.

As if the sound had awakened her and brought her back to reality, Genevieve tore her lips away from his. She brought her hand up to her mouth. Her eyes grew even bigger. Scared. "No," she whispered. "I absolutely can't do this."

Lucas recognized guilt the moment he saw it. He lived with it every day, and this moment, this day, would no doubt heap more guilt upon all that he already carried.

"You didn't do anything," he said. "I did. Please don't worry about this. Don't even think about it. It's all on me. I stepped well over the line. I apologize for touching you."

And because he was afraid that he might touch her again, scare her more, worry her more, he turned and walked away.

The truth was that he had done everything wrong with Genevieve from the start. He had hired her when he shouldn't have, given her too much work, not understood her situation, forced his will on her by making her move here, and now he had kissed her. His self-control had been compromised from day one.

That was going to have to stop. From now on he needed to realize that the two of them had to work in concert. Only by succeeding at this job and standing alone would she claim that independence she craved. Only by completing this task and moving on to the next and the next could he begin to make amends for his past transgressions. When this was over, she needed to move on. He needed that, too.

No more touching, he told himself. But he still craved another taste.

Genevieve stared in the mirror. She touched her aching lips. Something had happened back there with Lucas.

"A lot of somethings," she whispered. First of all, she had seriously messed up, allowing her daydreaming ways to get in the way of doing her job well. The room was a mess and she intended to fix it.

But more important than that was the other. Not the kiss. She wouldn't think about the kiss. It had been too overwhelming, too wonderful, too insane, too . . . everything. Thinking about kissing Lucas — or worse, kissing him *again* — would make her crazy. As it was, her nerves were tingling. If she hadn't somehow recalled herself, she would have been totally lost in his arms and then . . .

"Then, nothing, you idiot." Because that was what happened with Lucas. She'd been warned. Women tripped over each other trying to get to that incredible mouth of his and then he got tired of them. He moved on. Always. Always. And anyway, she did not want a man, did she?

"No, I can't want a man." Certainly not Lucas.

Yet here she was, doing what she had forbidden herself to do. Thinking about the kiss.

So Gen forced herself to remember the other, the way Lucas, a man who exuded power and control had been so angry at the thought that he might have harmed her that he let that famous control slip. She'd seen the pain behind the mask.

Lucas wasn't a man without feelings, as some thought. He was a man who didn't *want* to feel. He kept it bottled up. What had he said? That line about how a man like him should have learned how easy it was to hurt a woman? Apparently, he had regrets, bad memories of past relationships. He wasn't as cold as people said he was.

And there it was. Another brick in the wall that separated her from Lucas. Because if she fell in love with him and got hurt when he left her . . .

"I'll be a part of his pain," she said. Like Rita. Like . . . Angie? Was there a real Angie?

Don't think about it. Don't go there. And

don't get too close to him. It was immensely clear that any personal involvement between her and Lucas could only end up badly for both of them. Best to keep her distance.

A full hour after he had pulled Genevieve into his arms, Lucas was still agitated. He'd removed himself from the house to the yard, had taken off his jacket and was concentrating on splitting wood for the fireplaces for the winter. But the physical activity wasn't chasing away his irritation.

What had he been thinking? Lucas thought, slamming the ax into the wood so hard that the two halves flew across the yard. He never got involved with his employees; he certainly never had anything to do with potentially vulnerable women. Yet he had kissed Gen, a move that was surely only going to complicate things in major ways.

What was a man to do in such circumstances?

"Man up," he muttered, setting up another log and cleaving it cleanly in two. "Apologize."

But he'd already done that. It didn't feel like enough. The only thing to do now was move on. Never touch her again. Stop looking at her as a woman. At all.

Just do whatever you can to make this project move forward, make this project successful and get everything done and out of the way.

Then he would finally feel as if he deserved some small degree of absolution. By helping a few women forge a path back to happiness, he could find some solace.

But to do that he had to stop sidestepping time spent with Genevieve and just . . . get down to business. Surely if he kept his head down, his nose to the grindstone, and never touched her again, they could both walk away from this situation reasonably satisfied in just a few weeks.

CHAPTER SIX

Genevieve looked at her watch. Rats! She was running behind again. Ever since she'd moved in, ever since Lucas had kissed her, the two of them had been working at a feverish pace to finish everything before they opened the doors to Angie's House and Lucas moved on to France.

And until I . . . do what? she wondered. But there wasn't even time to worry about that. Thank goodness. Thinking about her future filled her with determination but also with trepidation and doubts. At least doing her job kept her mind off all that.

And off the memory of Lucas kissing her.

"Stop that," she ordered herself.

Out of the corner of her eye she caught Jorge looking at her, and she gave him a sheepish smile. "Sorry. Sometimes when I'm tense or rushed, I talk to myself."

He shrugged and returned her smile. "I noticed. You've been talking to yourself a lot lately. Lots of stress around here. Even Lucas has been talking to himself and that's not like him. I worked with him here when he opened one of his stores. I think this place —" Jorge gestured toward the wall "— means a lot to him. He told me it was special. I wonder if there really is an Angie. Why did he choose that name?"

"Maybe it's just a name, Jorge. And anyway, I'm sure that Lucas would have told us if he wanted us to know more." But she had wondered the same thing, she thought, as Jorge agreed and went on his way.

Truly she had wondered about whether there was an Angie too much, too often. Repeatedly. Especially since she knew that this was the first such project Lucas had taken on and he spoke of it with such fervor. Especially since she'd glimpsed that pain in his eyes. She hoped that all of the wondering she'd been doing didn't have anything to do with how Lucas had made her feel when he'd kissed her crazy.

Because that kiss couldn't matter. It was almost as if it had never happened in Lucas's eyes. Because once he'd apologized, he made it a point to keep his distance from her. He'd very politely told her that in order to speed up the project, she should feel free to use him in whatever way she needed to.

Then he'd given her a curt nod and walked away. Now, although they saw more of each other than they had in those first few days, they kept their personal interactions brief. Nonexistent, really.

He handled the financial end of things, some of the more technical aspects of structure. She handled the big picture, the "what do girls like?" items, the pizzazz end of things.

Those areas might have normally criss-crossed. They should have. Somehow, however, she and Lucas managed to keep a polite distance between them.

At least she hoped she gave the appearance of polite distance. She hoped he never caught her staring at his mouth or his chest and remembering how it had felt to be in his arms.

A buzzer went off at that moment, sending her thoughts flying. "Darn it," she said, looking at the reminder that appeared on her phone. She was supposed to be meeting with some of the neighbors over coffee tomorrow and she needed to finalize the food. That she could manage. The other item on her to-do list, sending out the invitations to the "meet the elite" party Lucas had requested was more problematic. Her throat closed up at the enormity of the task. The people he would want and expect might have come at her parents' calling. They wouldn't come for the "no artistic talent" daughter of the Patchetts. They especially wouldn't want to come to a party she was throwing if they had heard any of the rumors Barry had spread, and they surely had. Gossip expanded like bread dough in her parents' inner circle. She was going to fail Lucas.

For now she would concentrate on the coffee, the easy task. At least she'd thought it would be easy . . . until she showed up the next day and found herself fielding a barrage of questions.

"Would you consider marrying me? These cookies are better than any I've tasted and you're an extremely pretty lady. I think I'm in love." Those were the words Lucas heard as he entered the backyard where Genevieve was holding court with the neighbors. He glanced to where she was talking to a handsome aging man.

She was wearing a mischievous smile, and for a minute Lucas stood transfixed. It was hard to believe that any man — that rat ex-fiancé of hers — would intentionally hurt a woman like Gen. *But then, I've hurt plenty of women, haven't I?* And if he followed his inclinations and chased Genevieve's smiles, he would hurt her just like Barry had. Because in the end, he would still leave. And when they were done here, she needed her freedom and confidence, not some man born to disappoint her.

He leaned on the fence and listened.

"William, how many women have you asked to marry you today?" Genevieve said to the elderly man. "I'll bet it's been at least a dozen. But thank you so much for the compliment. If I could marry any man today, you'd be right at the top of my list. Unfortunately, I can't marry anyone. And I'll tell you a secret. I didn't bake the cookies. I bought them."

The man clapped one hand over his heart in mock horror. "No marriage? No home-baked cookies? Oh, you've broken my heart, Genevieve."

"I know. It's sad, but I'm sure another cookie or two will heal your heart. Even a store-bought cookie."

The man's laugh rang out, ending the exchange, and Genevieve moved on to another group of people. Lucas watched as she charmed them, keeping the conversation light. This was to be a social gathering only. Nothing serious. Just putting people's minds at ease by being friendly. He didn't really even have a place here, but she had asked him to stop by just in case anyone insisted on asking questions she couldn't answer.

"Genevieve, thank you for inviting us," one woman said. "This is so nice. I love all the pretty green and ivory umbrellas, and the food is delicious. I tell you, I'm glad to hear that you're happy with the size of the house. We were afraid someone was going to tear the place down and build something even bigger."

"No. The footprint will remain the same," Genevieve said, "and we'll make this pretty yard even more luscious by adding plenty of flowers and some benches."

"Will you be living here then, you and your husband?" the woman asked. "I told William there that the two of you were most likely married. Or going to be married. You both spend so much time here."

That was when Genevieve faltered. She looked up into Lucas's eyes, as if seeking him out. Or maybe she was just afraid that he had heard.

Slowly, she was shaking her head, that pretty blush spreading up her throat. For some totally foolish, insane reason Lucas couldn't understand, he wanted to hide her. He didn't want anyone other than himself to see that intimate color that disappeared beneath the collar of her blouse. Which was, of course, ridiculous. He had no more right to think intimate thoughts of Gen than anyone here.

"Lucas and I merely work together," Genevieve finally managed to say. "I suppose I should explain a bit about why we're here."

He couldn't help smiling. She was always so honest. The script called for a brief neighborhood social hour followed by a mailing and then another question-and-answer meeting, no explanations given today.

Well, so much for the script. This was a lot like Genevieve's foray into painting. Wild and uninhibited and . . . interesting. She was always interesting. And so were her cookies, he thought, looking down at the plates filled with miniature works of art.

But by then, she'd begun to speak. "This house is being transformed into a very special place," she began. "A place that will offer hope to people who need it very much and a place that will, I'm sure, be a credit to your wonderful, beautiful neighborhood."

"Hmm," one man said. "That sounds like a lead-in to something I'm not going to like. This is going to be some sort of home for people we won't want in our neighborhood, isn't it?"

Lucas frowned at the man. Maybe he even growled or took a step forward, because Genevieve immediately sent Lucas a pleading glance. Which did no good. All Lucas could think of was his mother, who had been a lost soul, of Angie, who had had abuse heaped upon her, of . . . Genevieve living in a place where there were bars on the windows. A man like that one could raise an outcry, turn people against this project, stop it from happening.

Stop Lucas from doing this thing he desperately needed and wanted to do. Lucas opened his mouth.

"I suppose that might be true," Genevieve said softly, halting Lucas's speech. "That is, if you think someone like me would be bad for the neighborhood. This home will be called Angie's House and it will house eight women like me. Ones who've had some hard times but want to raise themselves up. Women who need good, kind neighbors. Women who will work hard to win your trust and to become contributing members of the community."

She was putting words into the mouths of women she didn't even know and yet . . .

that *was* the goal of Angie's House, wasn't it?

For two seconds, she looked into Lucas's eyes. Was she looking for encouragement? He didn't know, but he nodded. Although what he really wanted to do was challenge any man who questioned her, he knew that wasn't what *she* wanted. Encouragement was all she would want to accept. *You're doing fine.* He tried to convey the words with his expression.

Which was ridiculous. He was not a sensitive man. He'd been told many times that he looked cold and foreboding. Reassurance wasn't in his library of expressions.

"So . . . are you Angie? Metaphorically, I mean," a woman asked.

"I don't know. Maybe I am."

"*Is* there a real Angie?"

"Must be. Why would they call it that if there wasn't an Angie?" a man said.

The questions came hard and fast, but most of them fixated on the name of the place. "Will the real Angie be coming here?" "Is she alive?" "Is she dead?" "Why did you call the place Angie's House? What's the story behind it?"

Lucas felt himself closing up inside. He cursed himself for not anticipating this. Of course, people would be curious about the significance of the name. What had he been thinking doing things this way?

And Genevieve . . . He'd put her in an uncomfortable position. She was supposed to be the all-knowing, all-seeing leader of this project and he had made her look bad by not giving her all the tools she needed.

"I —" She looked up. He thought she was going to look straight into his eyes, but just as her gaze almost met his, she quickly looked away. "I'm sorry. I don't know all the answers to your questions," she said. And she didn't promise that she would seek out the answers, either.

"So what do you know?" someone asked. "Tell us everything we need to know. This is our home."

Lucas saw the struggle on her face as she tried to decide what to tell, what would turn this back into a warm, friendly situation.

But at that moment, someone turned around and saw him leaning against the fence. "There's that guy. He probably knows more."

Lucas frowned. "I assure you, Genevieve is the person to answer your questions."

"But she doesn't know all the answers."

"You're wrong about that. She knows all the answers."

"She didn't know who Angie was."

Lucas stared the man down. "She was protecting me, shielding my feelings. Angie was —" he took a deep breath "— a woman I once cared for."

"Will she be coming here? Is she still alive? Did she die a tragic death?"

"Donald, that's enough. The man obviously suffered a personal tragedy and it's none of our business," a woman who must have been his wife said.

The man made a rude noise. "He named this place after her. This is our neighborhood. That makes it our business. Why should we, the neighbors, be the last to know?"

The man had a point. There were people who deserved to know the story. Genevieve should know.

"Angie isn't alive, I'm afraid. She won't be coming here." Somehow he managed to keep his voice on an even keel. He managed not to look at Genevieve, because he was afraid that he would read pity in her eyes. "Are there any more questions?"

"If there are, I'll take over from here, Lucas . . . ? Perhaps our neighbors would like to get a glimpse of what I've done with the ground floor."

"You don't want to miss this," he told the crowd. "Genevieve has a way of looking at a space, envisioning the people who will be occupying it and turning the place into something magical." He stared at her as he said it. He meant every word. She had . . . a gift. And no matter what had happened here today, he wouldn't let that gift be overlooked because what was to have been a social gathering had turned down a sad path.

Genevieve looked back at him. "Thank you," she said. "Thank you so much." Then with a sad smile and a firm step, Genevieve led the group away.

Lucas was left alone with his naked reality. He'd wanted to do some good while keeping his past private. Now the world would know his anguish. They'd pity him, and he had sworn — long ago — that he would never be an object of pity again. He needed . . .

Genevieve, he thought for one insane moment. But only for one moment. Then he went inside to a room in the attic where he kept a few things. What he needed couldn't be Genevieve. What he needed was to reclaim his sanity, his control, his life, to get things back on an even keel. Rebuild the walls, practice discipline.

One hundred push-ups later, he was ready to talk to Genevieve.

■ ■ ■ ■

Genevieve stood staring up into Lucas's dark eyes, eyes that had looked anguished only a short time ago. How had she not anticipated what would happen? How could she have let him bare his soul that way? She was supposed to be the project manager, in charge of the whole deal. "Lucas, I'm so sorry about what happened earlier. I should have been prepared with an answer, some light response, something to deflect the questions. I take total responsibility."

He took a step closer, the expression in his eyes more dangerous than she'd ever seen before. "Are you . . . implying that you should have protected me, Genevieve?"

She lifted her chin. "I should have reviewed all the possibilities." It was one of her parents' biggest complaints, that her views were not large enough. Her world wasn't large enough. They worked on big canvasses. She did not.

"Even the possibility that there would be questions I had given you no answers to?"

"Even that."

"Don't do that," he ordered.

"Don't do what?"

"Don't take the blame for things you can't

be blamed for. I'm the one who should be apologizing to you. I left you there hanging in the breeze. I let them sucker punch you with their questions about Angie."

She shook her head slowly. "That wasn't your fault."

"It was. I'm the one who picked the darn name and I know all too well how harsh people can be when it comes to anyone who is different or poor or in need."

And there it was. That look. The one that told her everything and nothing. The one she had no business wondering about.

"What happened to you? And who is Angie, really?" she asked suddenly.

The minute she said the words she clapped her hand over her mouth. Lucas was her boss. If he had wanted her to know these things . . .

"I'm sorry."

"Don't be. I told you once that if you wanted to know anything that you should ask."

"You were talking about my work."

"Yes, but now it seems that my life has overflowed into your work. And what happened to me was . . . a lot of things a long time ago. A mother who wanted to be a dancer, but who got pregnant and always felt that my birth destroyed her career. I

134

broke her heart over and over and she struggled to love me . . . until she gave up and left. Then my father died and I moved from one foster family to the next. Some of them just wanted to rack up accolades for taking in a troubled kid. They never kept me long. I was wild, angry, virtually uncontrollable and I kicked out at them as much as I could. Finally, I ended up on the streets. Then, when I was eighteen, I met Louisa."

He said the name as if it had significance. Genevieve waited.

"Louisa Ensen was Angie's real name. Angie was just a code name we used because her father was a violent man and he hated me. Whenever I called, if he answered, I'd disguise my voice and ask for Angie or get someone else to ask for her. His grumbling about the constant wrong numbers was Louisa's cue that I was waiting for her to meet me."

"I don't understand," Genevieve said. "You said that she was dead."

Lucas looked to the side. It was one of the few times when he'd ever avoided making eye contact with her. "Once things take off with this place, if anyone knew there really was a real, living Angie . . . I don't want anyone trying to find her. I named the shelter for her because of what happened,

135

as a kind of . . . apology. But she deserves some peace, some privacy."

He looked up then, staring directly into Genevieve's eyes. His expression was . . . terrible, cold. "She came to me one night. Her father was in a rage and she just needed a few minutes away. But even though I knew what he was like, I asked her to stay with me. So she stayed. Because she trusted me and because I made her feel safe. Because of me, she got home incredibly late.

"Two days later she called and told me that she didn't want to see me anymore. She said she'd met someone else, someone better, with money and class, someone who wasn't always in trouble.

"I was so angry and hurt that I couldn't see straight and I left town right away. Louisa became just one more woman who had betrayed me. That was when I gave up on people and concentrated on work, on learning how to discipline myself and control my situations, how to make money. I never looked back. In a way, Louisa freed me to make a better life for myself. Then just under a year ago I ran into her in Albany. She was cleaning rooms at a hotel where I was staying, and the minute she recognized me, she tried to walk away. When she turned, I saw that she had a long scar running down her cheek, an old one. And I knew right away what had happened."

"Her father beat her, didn't he?" Genevieve couldn't keep the horror from her voice.

Lucas's entire body radiated tension, anger. "He didn't just beat her. He nearly killed her. That long-ago night when she went home, her father knew she'd been with me and he hit her until he she couldn't even stand up, until she couldn't recognize herself in the mirror. He told her that he'd kill me if I ever came near her again. So, she sent me away, and I made it so . . . easy. Too easy. I was the one who had asked her to stay with me, the one who was responsible for the torture he put her through, and because of my crime, I left town and became a millionaire while she stayed and took all the punishment alone.

"She walks with a limp now. She never got married, never found any happiness. When she saw how I had prospered when she had suffered . . . I don't know how she could forgive me, but for some reason she has."

Genevieve's heart lurched. She wanted to tell him that Louisa forgave him because he'd done nothing wrong, but . . . he *had* done something wrong. He'd asked Louisa to stay, knowing that her father flew into rages. No platitudes she could offer would change that in his mind.

"You were very young," she said anyway.

He swore. "And I'd lived the life of a much older person. I knew all about people who liked to attack the weak. I asked her to stay with me and she took the risk, but she also paid the price. I didn't."

Oh, that was so wrong. He was paying the price even now.

"So, this house," Genevieve said, "is to make amends."

He gave a harsh laugh. "Nothing makes amends for something like that. She was robbed of her beauty and youth and her life. She'll never get any of that back, but . . . she has a daughter now. Not mine, but a daughter by a man as evil as her father. She ran from him to protect her child. She was barely making ends meet when our paths crossed.

"So I forced money on her, but money can't cure the things that scare her. Her daughter will be ten the day that Angie's House opens. When we were young, she often talked about a safe place, a dream place. I want this to be a gift for her. If she or her child ever need an Angie's House, I want there to be one for them. All she wanted was someplace she could live a normal life, free to dream the kinds of dreams that other girls dreamed. And that's what this is about. But to the world? Angie is dead. Can you handle that?"

Genevieve's throat was closing up. He had planned the opening of Angie's House as a gift to a child he'd never even met and most likely never would. He was protecting the woman he felt he'd harmed.

Oh, she knew what he was asking. "You want me to lie," she said.

"I know. I'm sorry to even ask this favor of you, but . . . yes. Can you make that lie stick, please? For Angie?"

Genevieve didn't know Angie even though she felt for her. But she knew one thing. "I can lie," she promised. She would do it for Lucas.

Suddenly he smiled and it felt as if the sun had exploded into the room. As if a part of her heart she hadn't known she owned began to beat. "You should smile more often," she said, then blushed at her own audacity. "I'll learn to lie, Lucas," she promised again. "I'll practice until I get it right."

His smile dimmed a bit. "Don't let me corrupt you, Gen," he said, his voice low and fierce.

"I won't," she whispered. "I won't." But he was close, so close. She took a step. So did he. Then she was in his arms, and she didn't know whether he was corrupting her or she was corrupting him, but there was kissing going on. Her lips against his, his arms pulling her closer, an ache so sweet she thought she might die from it.

Then he was pulling away. "I don't want to hurt you, Genevieve."

She knew what he was telling her. He never stayed; he never loved. He'd hurt other women and he would always live with that guilt. He didn't want to have her on his conscience, too.

"You can't hurt me," she told him, even though she suspected that he could hurt her very badly. Already it seemed, she was learning how to lie. "I'm an independent woman. No man can have me or hold me, remember?"

And that was the truth. That was what she wanted. It was going to become her mantra. If control was what gave Lucas's life meaning, then independence would be her saving grace.

Now, more than ever, she wanted to do this job right. For so many reasons.

Then, just to prove to Lucas that she was unaffected by his kisses and to show herself that she could survive those kisses, she rose on her tiptoes, wrapped her arms around his neck and pressed her lips to his again.

"I'm not going to fail you ever, Lucas," she said. "I'll give this party and Angie's House everything I have." Then she returned to her office to begin on the plans she'd put off for too long.

She only hoped that when this was all over and Lucas had gone, she would be able to leave him with a smile. This time when Lucas moved on, she wanted things to be different. She wanted him to have a happy farewell with no regrets and no guilt.

It sounded so simple, so doable. And yet . . . already she wanted to be back in his arms.

"Get over it, Gen," she ordered herself. But she didn't get over it. Maybe later.

CHAPTER SEVEN

Lucas could hardly believe that he'd bared his soul to Genevieve. He'd never told that story to anyone. Ever. He wasn't sure how he felt about having shared so much. Like a jerk who had dumped too much emotional baggage on Genevieve? Exposed too much of himself? Yes to both of those.

Still, she'd needed to know the whole story, he reasoned. For her job. And maybe because hearing about his fouled-up past might give her a shot of confidence. If someone who'd been as messed up as he had could go on to experience success, think what she could do. She could harness the moon and make it her own. All she needed was that one key to unlock the fire that burned within her.

And he knew it was there. The flame that she carried inside glowed. He'd seen it when she was charming the neighbors. It burned him every time he touched her, every single time her lips met his.

Still, ever since he'd shared that story and she had sworn to give the "introduce potential sponsors" party her all, she'd been running full tilt, planning, ripping up the plans, starting over again, nervously trying to get the wording on the invitations just right. Berating herself. And she had continued to decorate and do the messier jobs, too.

"It soothes me," she said. Today she was trying to apply wallpaper to a small sitting room. Jorge had given her basic instructions, but from the sounds that were coming from the room, Lucas was pretty sure things weren't going according to plan.

He peered around the corner. And immediately frowned. As time had passed and Genevieve had messed up her more useful clothes — if one could call anything she owned useful — her wardrobe had devolved . . . or evolved, depending on a man's attitude. Her remaining "work" outfits were becoming less and less appropriate for all the bending, stretching, and crawling around on the floor she was doing as she measured, reached and generally went into full-immersion designer mode.

The other day it had been a gauzy blouse with a form-fitting chemise beneath that had cupped her breasts in such a way that he had barely been able to tear his eyes away. Today, this silky thing was making him imagine the material sliding beneath his fingertips as he removed it and —

A frustrated growl escaped him.

"Lucas? What's wrong?" Genevieve looked up from the strip of wallpaper she was wrestling into place. He took one look at it and knew that it wasn't going to stick. At least not straight. The paper was already half-mangled. There was no way he was going to be the one to give her the disappointing news, not when she was so good at blaming herself. She needed a distraction. *He* needed a distraction, some way to keep from thinking about kissing her, touching her, inviting her to his bed. Any of those would be a tremendous mistake for a man who measured his success by how well he maintained self-control. And he wouldn't be doing Gen any favors, either, when she had already told him she was on the run from overbearing, overcontrolling men. Men like him.

"What's wrong?"

Too much.

"Nothing at all," he said. "I just thought that I'd take you shopping." Her silky blouse clung to her body in ways that made his temperature rise, and Lucas forced himself to keep his distance. "Let's do that today. Now."

Genevieve blinked. "You want to take me shopping? I assume you must mean . . . for food for the party? Don't worry. I've got that part under control. I'm having it catered." But he noticed that she frowned when she said that. She was still uncertain if anyone would show up for a Patchett daughter.

"Don't you think you need some clothes? Practical clothes for this . . . painting, cleaning, wallpapering, since you seem determined to keep doing all those things. You can't keep wearing things that —"

Drive me crazy. Make me think about kissing you, touching you.

He frowned and noticed that once again, she had torn something. There was a small hole in the thigh of her slacks.

She sighed and stepped away from the wallpaper. "I know. This looks silly, doesn't it?" She looked down at herself.

"It looks fantastic. You look fantastic, but once this job is over . . . you'll want your clothes to last. You need jeans. We need to buy you some. You might need all your dressier stuff for your next job and you won't want everything to be paint splattered or torn."

And for the life of him, he couldn't look away from that tiny rip in her slacks. Her creamy skin was barely visible, the hole was so small, but his imagination was very fertile.

"That's a problem," he muttered and he wasn't referring to the rip but to his own obsession with it. "Let's fix that."

Gen's heart was banging like a pair of cymbals. Lucas was staring at the tiniest, hardly noticeable hole in her pants, the one she'd been sure no one would ever even key in on, and it felt as if he was seeing a lot more of her skin than he was. Automatically, she started to cover the rip with her hand, then stopped when she decided that the move was unnecessary. *Come on, Gen. The hole's barely the size of a diamond chip. You're probably just imagining that he's staring at it.*

But the minute she forced her mind away from thoughts of having Lucas stare at her naked skin, the reality of what he was asking her to do kicked in. Shopping. Walking into stores. Facing the people who had been key players in witnessing her total humiliation. The humiliation she'd been hyperventilating about all this week while she'd been trying to plan this party. Only . . . shopping would take her directly to the source of where the most awful thing had happened.

Her heart started beating hard all over again. Too fast. "I — I'd really rather *not* go shopping."

Lucas frowned.

"I mean, there's so much to do here," she insisted, her words practically falling over themselves. "Besides, I still have lots of clothes, so buying more is really not necessary and —"

"Genevieve. Stop."

She stopped.

He stepped closer. "What's wrong? Why are you suddenly so flustered? What did I say? Tell me."

Oh, no, he thought he was the one at fault. "It isn't you, Lucas. I just . . . I just can't go shopping. I can't. Please."

If a man could have looked more confused, Genevieve wasn't sure what he would look like.

"You're going to need to explain why you're making a simple shopping excursion sound like a prison sentence."

She sighed. "That first day when you said you'd checked my background, I thought you knew all about me, but apparently you only knew about my work history or lack of it. There's more."

"Gen, I wouldn't have gone digging into your personal secrets. Some things are off-limits." His voice was low and deep and soothing, and she couldn't help looking up into his eyes.

She nodded, tightly. "Thank you," she said, her voice too small. "But given the situation, you probably need to know this next part. When my parents died, I had no clue how to go on about things, but I thought I didn't have to worry because Barry, who was my fiancé as well as my parents' financial advisor, was taking care of all the details. What I didn't know was that he had been slowly stealing my parents' money and now that they were gone, he didn't need to marry me for the rest of it. All he had to do was to take advantage of my ignorance.

"While I was trying to sort out my life and not paying attention, he was making it appear that I was going on totally irresponsible and extravagant shopping sprees. I apparently bought lots of things, tons of frivolous items, on the internet and over the phone and he even sent my employees, my house-keeper and a maid, to the stores to buy things in my name. He dropped in little hints about my splurges to my friends and acquaintances. He took me shopping and managed to make it look as if, without my parents' guidance, I was out of control and buying things that eventually ended up in his possession."

She hazarded a glance at Lucas, who was looking like a dark thundercloud. "You don't have to tell me this," he said.

"I know. I want to." She rushed on, afraid she wouldn't be able to finish if she didn't get it all out at once. "Of course, the amount of money I was supposedly throwing away was small compared to what he was siphoning off on the side, but the story served its purpose as camouflage. By the time my fortune was gone and he had disappeared, leaving no trace of what he had done or where he had gone, everyone thought that I was an out-of-control shopping addict and a spoiled rich brat who had run through her parents' fortune. I believe there were even rumors that some of my money went for drugs. I'm not sure I ever even realized all the lies that he fabricated about me.

"But when he was finished . . . he had apparently been quite convincing. I still remember going into a store on a legitimate errand and having my credit card denied, because there was no more money. That was how I found out. It was a store where everyone knew me. I gave them another card and had the same results. Then, I tried to ask questions, to plead my innocence, but the pitying, disgusted looks the clerks and the other shoppers gave me and the comments they made were . . ." Genevieve shuddered. "I don't like to shop anymore and I restrict my excursions to the basics. Mostly food. All the rest . . . I became an embarrassment to my friends and acquaintances. I like nice things, but I'm fine with what I already have, thank you."

Lucas's dark gaze was almost brutal. "If your friends considered you an embarrassment because they fell for a con man's lies, then those friends weren't worth keeping. Especially when you were blameless."

"I wasn't blameless. I was an idiot. This is the twenty-first century — I'm a modern woman. Yet, I let Barry make all the decisions and didn't question a thing."

"Everyone trusts the wrong person now and then."

Genevieve wondered who Lucas had trusted. He no longer trusted that deeply and probably never would. He probably would never have shared his Angie story with her yesterday if he hadn't felt that she, as project manager, would need to have ready answers for the inevitable questions.

"Maybe if I had a history of being accomplished and independent and smart about money and people, I and everyone else could simply write off my situation as merely an anomaly, one mistake in a sea of good decisions. But I don't have that strong history. I had lived my whole life with my parents, doing their bidding, a bit like a ventriloquist's puppet. I made it easy for people to think I was the kind of person who would flip out and go wild when I got my first taste of freedom."

"Public humiliation cuts deep and I can't tell you how to handle your situation, Genevieve, but whenever my pride has taken a blow, I've found that facing my opponents down is the best thing to do," he said.

Because of what he'd told her yesterday, she knew this wasn't just garden-variety well-meaning advice he was giving her. As a child, he'd been hurt by the very people who should have cared for him, repeatedly. He'd had people he loved turn their backs on him. It was so much more than his pride that had been damaged.

"How did you do it?" she asked softly. "How did you survive all that and come out a serious winner? You always look so confident."

He shrugged as if it was nothing, but

she'd heard his voice go thick yesterday. It hadn't been nothing. He'd simply learned to control his outward reactions, not his memories.

"Don't give me any trophies, Genevieve. I haven't done anything anyone else couldn't do. It's all about appearances, training your body to project confidence. With a bit of practice, you can mask the memory of that hurt and make people see only what you want them to see. No one will ever know that a jerk of a man once stole something precious from you."

He was frowning intensely. She knew he wasn't talking about the money. And he had her half-convinced this lesson was all about changing her life . . . until she remembered how she'd felt that day. Like a shoplifter, a fraud, a cheat.

"Don't look like that," he warned.

"Like what?"

"Like you're going to make up an excuse to back out on me. This conversation might have started with me wanting you to buy some jeans but now that I know just how much of a jerk Barry was, this little shopping trip is about so much more. I certainly wouldn't mind helping you get back some of your own. Wouldn't you like to walk into that store where everyone gave you those sneering looks and give them the queen treatment?"

"The queen treatment?"

"The 'you may kiss my hand' looks."

Genevieve sucked in a breath. "I never did that, even when I had money."

"Somehow that doesn't surprise me. Still, it's important to get back on your horse and ride when you've had a spill. Didn't you tell me that you intended to be your own woman, beholden to no one?"

"I do."

"Gen, as far as you've come, as much as you've accomplished running the show here at Angie's House, you'll still never be the woman you want to be if you're terrified of walking into a store for fear that everyone will think that you'll lose control or that they'll throw you out because you have no money."

"I have money," she said. "You paid me."

He smiled. "Exactly."

"I'm still not sure about this."

"I am. Consider it the next step to reclaiming your independence."

And how could she argue with that? Her independence was all that mattered, wasn't it? The fact that Lucas smiled at her in a way that made her heart start misbehaving was immaterial. She hoped. As long as she didn't pay attention to her heart, she should be all right. Shouldn't she?

So, Genevieve hadn't had an easy time this past year, Lucas mused as he watched her purchase the one pair of jeans and one blouse she had insisted was all she needed. She'd lost everything she'd once had, including the people who had loved her; she'd had a jerk of a fiancé who had totally betrayed her. And she was completely alone. She'd been kicked around.

He knew what that was like. After his mother's desertion, his father's death, being cast off by foster parent after foster parent, he'd had to scramble to stay afloat emotionally. He'd been betrayed and he'd learned to be the betrayer; he'd gotten mean, but he knew that some people, innocent people like Angie or Genevieve, weren't ever going to be the mean type. They were easy prey, easily hurt.

She had no experience with the tough stuff that had been handed to her, and so she was like a defenseless puppy some idiot had decided to torture. And he hated that. That must be why he had a raw need to see Genevieve reclaim her pride.

Watching her now, he couldn't help feeling . . . good, proud, exultant. She had, at his suggestion, very publicly paraded around the store, trying on many pairs of jeans before eventually settling on the ones she'd chosen in the first five minutes.

"If they think you're out of control with a charge card, lead them on a little by putting on a show. Then you'll prove them wrong and get back a little of your own when you make only a modest purchase," he suggested. "Never give them what they expect. You want to be the one who retains control of the situation. By bobbing and weaving and doing the unexpected — like a prize-fighter — you'll never let them have a chance to hurt you." Now she was putting words to deeds.

"Just these two items," she said to the salesperson, holding out the debit card Lucas had provided for her.

The woman at the register looked at the name on the card, then quietly excused herself and went away. In search of a manager, he was sure. Obviously, Genevieve's name was on a list of those with less than optimum credit ratings. To Gen's credit, even though he could tell that she was incredibly self-conscious and uncomfortable, she stood tall, no hint of her inner turmoil on her usually expressive face. She waited, pretending to look at other items he knew she had no intention of buying. Eventually, the sales clerk returned.

"I'm sorry this took so long," the woman said. "Computer problems today, you know."

"Is there . . . a problem with the card?" Genevieve asked, sweetly, staring directly at the woman as he had told her to do.

The woman looked away slightly, then shook her head. "No, not at all. It went through with no trouble. Thank you for your business, Ms. Patchett." She bagged the purchases and handed the bag to Genevieve. "Come back soon."

Genevieve flashed her an impish smile, but she didn't commit to anything. When she and Lucas were outside the store, she let out a long breath. "Okay, tell me, what did I buy? I was too nervous to pay much attention."

He chuckled. "I don't believe you for a minute, but I applaud you. No one could have told that you were nervous. You handled yourself well, and no one looked down their noses at you."

She smiled. "I never thought that shopping could become such an intimidating experience, but then I never thought about a lot of things until this year. I lived a very protected life, I think." She wrinkled her nose.

"Nothing wrong with living a sheltered life."

"Except it keeps you from learning how to actually live and take care of yourself. But that's all behind me now. Soon I'll be a fully armored female. Invincible. Able to handle any situation. Thank you for the pep talk and the lesson. You knew just what you were talking about."

He shrugged. "I learned early in life how to stick my chin out and stare people in the eye, even when it would have been smarter to back down."

She stopped and stared at him. Uh-oh, he shouldn't have said that. "Those foster parents you had, the ones who walked away . . . what did they do when you stared them in the eye?"

Oh, no, he knew that look. He'd seen it a thousand times, and he had always hated it. It was the "let me make you my next pet project" look.

"Nothing you need to worry about. I'm not a boy anymore."

She opened her mouth as if to argue.

"Seriously. Don't say anything," he said, and without thinking he placed his fingertips over her lips. Bad mistake. Her mouth was soft, warm, incredibly tempting.

"I won't," she promised, ignoring his command to stay quiet. Her movement sent that pretty mouth sliding against the pads of his fingers. He wanted to groan. Instead, he smiled as he pulled away from her.

"What?" she asked.

"Do you often do the opposite of what you're told?"

Genevieve blinked. "Actually, I spent most of my life doing exactly as I was told. My parents were very absorbed in their work. They wanted a quiet, well-behaved child who would fade into the background and not be a bother, and I complied. I think I thought that if I did everything they asked of me, maybe they would notice me, even love me. But hey, you can't have everything you want, can you?" She smiled, a brave smile, as if trying to comfort *him* for having to listen to her misfortune.

A black mist seized his soul. It was one thing for someone like him who had kicked his way out of the womb, fists swinging, and who had continued to fight the world, to be denied love. He had fought, sworn, stolen, run away and generally been trouble to everyone. He'd deserted Angie in her hour of need. He didn't deserve love. But someone soft and earnest like Genevieve?

158

He wanted her to win, to have what she needed.

She looked at him with those big green eyes full of hope.

He groaned. He fought himself. And then he lost control. He pulled her into his arms, plunging his fingers into her hair as he kissed her. "Why do you hide your beautiful hair like this?" he grumbled, but he didn't wait for her to answer. Her mouth called to him and he had to taste her again.

She was sweet, she was heaven in his arms, her curves against his body. He wanted more of her. And he got what he wanted when she returned his kiss.

He pulled her closer, kissed her more. Then he pulled away. "I'm not going to be like Barry," he said. "I want you. I want *this* from you. But I'm not going to overstep the bounds. I don't want to be another man you'll regret when I'm gone. I'm not a part of your plans."

"You're not," she agreed, her palms resting lightly against his chest, making him crazy, testing his self-control. "You're not in my plans. No man is. But . . ."

He waited.

"But sometimes you're in my fantasies," she whispered as she rose on her toes and kissed him again. "I try to control those, because I'm sure it would be a mistake to kiss you too often."

And that night she was in his fantasies, too. As she had been ever since he'd met her. It didn't change a thing. Genevieve was coming off of a major hurt. Two major hurts if you included her genius parents, who had been clueless about caring for a child. He wasn't going to be another person hurting her. For her sake. And his. He didn't think he could take damaging another person. Especially not Gen.

Besides, he wasn't in her plans. Never would be. He needed to keep that in mind.

CHAPTER EIGHT

A week later Genevieve stood in the gold-and-white banquet room of Lucas's hotel, shifting her weight from one foot to the other. Any moment now, people were going to start filing through the doors. Or at least she hoped they would. She was almost ready to faint from the tension, wondering if people would come out of curiosity or stay away because, after all, who *was* she? Not her artist parents by a long shot. Not anyone important, really. She ran her hands down the slender lines of her strapless pale blue sheath, trying to calm herself, to appear poised. As if that was even possible.

And Lucas? He looked cool as ever in formal black and white, totally uninvolved. But by now Genevieve was beginning to know him a bit better. This project meant a lot to him. The fact that he was hiding the tension he must be feeling was just a testament to how well he'd trained himself. He always had his finger on the control button.

Except when he kisses a woman. Then he loses it. The thought just dropped right in there, catching Genevieve by surprise. Was she blushing? She must be blushing. Lucas was looking concerned.

"Everything looks fantastic, Gen. You outdid yourself. The framed photos you took of Angie's House look superb. The room, the food, the wine . . . it's all perfect. I hope you know that, so there's nothing to worry about. We're just going to wade right in and do this thing, all right? We're going to make it happen."

She nodded, aware that her focus felt different tonight. In the space of a few weeks she'd gone from simply wanting a job in order to save herself to needing to help Lucas. Because this charity was his salvation. The stakes had been upped. And the fact that she cared so much about his part of the outcome tonight . . . ?

She wasn't going to even examine that scary thought. "I just hope that the invitations I sent out were enough to attract some curiosity seekers."

He smiled although it wasn't the full-bodied smile he had gifted her with the other day. "I especially liked the part of the invitation where you referred to 'some previously unseen' Patchett art. Very provocative."

Genevieve took a deep breath. "Yes, well I might have stretched the limits a bit with that one. There really isn't any previously unseen art. At least none that my parents would have allowed anyone to display in a gallery. I have a few things they hadn't gotten around to trashing when they died. If they knew I was doing this, they would come back to life just to berate me for it." She nodded toward a display area she had set up in the middle of the room. There were a few drawings, a few sculptures, some glasswork and a stack of their notes concerning projects they hadn't gotten around to starting. "Not very interesting stuff to an aficionado and yet it was the only draw I could think of. Moreover . . ."

He waited.

"I'm not an artist, but I spent a lot of time listening at art shows. My parents were very good at what they did, most of the time, but sometimes they talked up their pieces in such a way that people thought the work was even better than it actually was. I'm counting on that sort of scenario this time, hoping the guests will see what they want to see rather than the reality. If they don't, we're sunk. They'll just get angry at the misrepresentation and refuse to back any project we're involved in. What will happen if no one steps forward tonight and offers to sponsor another project?"

He breathed in a deep, tight, long breath. "I can still manage to fund and staff one or two more projects."

But she already knew that he wanted and needed to do more. This initial project was the mother ship, but there were women all over the country who needed a place to heal and grow. They had become his penance, a way to get over his past.

"So, we'll just have to get more donors tonight," she said, closing her eyes and trying not to let the pressure get to her. She'd never sold anyone on anything in her life.

He gently placed his fingertips on her bare arm. "Gen, stop pressuring yourself. You've gone above and beyond what anyone could ask for in organizing this event and you've come up with a stellar guest list. If you think I'm going to blame you if people choose to be less than generous with their checkbooks tonight, you're wrong."

"I don't think that." Even though it was what her parents would have done. When a gallery opening didn't go well, they had always been ready with plenty of criticism for the nonartist in the family, the one who must have messed something up. But Lucas? He wasn't like that. He was even letting her off the hook for the most demanding part of the night because he thought she would feel like a failure if the evening didn't go well.

Because you're standing here with your eyes closed, taking deep breaths, you idiot. No wonder he's worried about you. You're talking about a man who feels he failed his mother because he was a difficult child. He thinks he drove foster parents out of the system because he was too out of control. His formative years were spent being told that he was too horrible to love. And he can't forgive himself for what happened to Louisa. So, do not be a ninny and become one more woman on the list in his guilt book. Which was what would happen if she didn't get her act together.

It was what would happen if she did something stupid like falling in love with him.

The very thought made her heart hurt. She opened her eyes. There was no way she was going to let herself fall for Lucas and become another regret for him.

And darn it, she *did* want to do more, to try to help him turn this night into a success. So . . . what could she do? How could she make a difference? How could she take that bravado she'd accessed in that store the other day and apply it to this situation? *Think, Gen, think.* What did she know about art shows and patrons and her parents?

A tiny hint of an idea came to her. A crazy idea. A scary idea.

"Genevieve? What are you thinking? You're frowning."

"Don't worry. I'm just concentrating. I've hired people to man the tables, hand out literature and take donations. That's their part. The women will flock around you, and you'll charm them. That's your part."

He raised that lazy, wicked brow of his. She told herself the gesture wasn't sexy at all . . . even though it was. Very sexy. "I see."

She wanted to keep this light, so she patted him on the cheek.

"Good," she said, eliciting a killer smile from him. "Yes, I'm sure you'll be good at that. They'll probably be fighting for the privilege of writing the first check. As for me, I —"

"Will charm the men?" He frowned.

She did, too. "Not likely. Given my past associations with most of our guests tonight, I don't have the ability to swing the favor of these people to our side, not on my own. But I finally realized that I do have one possible weapon."

"What is it?"

She took a deep breath. "It might not work. It's a long shot, but . . . the thing is, I've spent a lot of my life sitting in corners, behind flower arrangements and I've walked around passing out drinks at occasions like these. I've been the fly on the wall countless times. So while I can't wow the guests the way my parents did, I do know their weaknesses. Every single one of them wants the last cookie on the plate, the thing that no one else can have."

"I take it you have the last cookie?"

"I do." She gestured toward the display of her parents' work. "Let's just hope that all those art classes I took can help me sell them on the concept that even an inferior Patchett work is better than most artists' best work. And that if I can get them in the mood to buy art, they'll make the leap and also contribute to a good cause. I've never tried to do this, you understand, but tonight . . ." Her voice trailed off. What was she thinking? She was totally out of her league here, wasn't she?

"You're willing to do that, to chat up the very people who snubbed you, the ones who believed the lies? Gen, these are people you knew and I know they hurt you. It's different from confronting a store clerk you'll never see again. You don't have to do this."

She knew, and the fact that he cared whether she got hurt . . . her heart just ached. And she had to wonder . . . was she approaching that fine line between women Lucas wanted and women he felt he'd wronged? Was there even a line or just a cliff face that fell away on each side?

Either way, the glaring truth was that she and Lucas together was a bad idea. She felt a little heartsick, a little queasy, a feeling that only grew stronger when she saw the first guests filtering in. They were people she recognized and yes . . . people she feared. But people who could help Lucas.

She gave a tight nod and tried to smile up at him. "Don't worry about me. I'm doing it. Most of the people who'll be here tonight didn't snub me, since we never had the opportunity to meet in person once my parents were gone. It was the younger crowd, their children, who did the honors. Besides, even if these people tonight believed the lies they heard about me, a very wise man I know taught me how to hold my head up and confront the people who made me uncomfortable. And yes, it's not quite the same as standing up to a salesperson, but . . ."

He waited.

"I could use a pep talk from my boss. How about a few kind words?" She tried out a teasing tone, wanting to keep this light.

Apparently, he did, too. "I believe in you," he said.

She smiled.

"And I like your hair like that." He touched a soft auburn curl. She had left it loose tonight.

"Now you've gone too far in trying to build up my confidence before I face the dragons. Red hair of this shade is jarring."

"Dragons?" He grinned. "That's an apt way of putting things, and no I'm not lying. Your hair is amazing — the color is striking and beautiful. It garners attention. In the best way possible." His sexy whisper felt as if it slithered right down through her body, touching her . . . everywhere, and just when she thought she might shiver with forbidden delight, a cough sounded near her elbow.

Genevieve turned to see Alvin Bevin, a very wealthy man. His daughter had led the charge in ridiculing Genevieve after the shopping incident.

It took Gen a few seconds to unfreeze her face and body.

"Are either of you the hosts?" he asked. "I'm —"

"Mr. Bevin," Genevieve said, a bit too loud. "I'm so glad to see you again."

He looked perplexed.

"I'm Genevieve Patchett," she said, feeling as if she'd fallen into a nightmare. None of these people were going to know her. It was going to be a long night.

"Oh, yes, I remember now," he said, and it was clear that he remembered the tales of how she'd blasted her way through her fortune. Immediately, his interest seemed to wane. He obviously thought her beneath contempt for throwing away what her parents had spent years amassing.

Lucas cleared his throat. For a moment, Genevieve thought he was going to step in and try to rescue her. He looked as if he wanted to, but he merely waited.

"Mr. Bevin, allow me to introduce you to Lucas McDowell of McDowell Sporting Goods. He's our host tonight."

It was as if she'd just told Alvin that he'd gotten a free pass into heaven. She'd seldom seen the older man smile, but he smiled broadly now. "McDowell Sporting Goods' stores? One of my favorite places. Just . . . could I ask you a question? It's about drivers and how to correct my golf swing."

Uh-oh, this could go so wrong, but . . . interrupting a man who wanted to discuss his golf swing, something that clearly was of great importance to him? Not a good idea.

I'm plunging in, anyway, she thought. "Mr. Bevin, I'm so sorry to interrupt at such a critical moment, but I promised Lucas I'd show him my parents' secret work and we were just about to go look at it. Would you like to come along? The party is so young that I don't think anyone else has had a chance to go over there yet."

"Secret work? Why . . . yes."

She felt Lucas smile, actually felt it even though she wasn't looking at him. And then, when they all headed toward the display, she could swear that an unseen hand touched her hair.

Fire shot through her. Either her imagination was running way too hot where Lucas was concerned, or he had wanted to offer her some encouragement, a high five by hair. At any rate, her confidence level rose. Alvin Bevin was hers. She wasn't letting him go until he agreed to be a sponsor for Angie's House. She knew just the piece that he would be interested in seeing, too.

But taking him directly to the treasure wouldn't do. She had to show him all the things he wouldn't want first, build up to the prize that would, hopefully, get him to make the leap to being a sponsor.

"Here are some of my father's paintings. Still lifes, mostly," she said.

Alvin grunted, looked and shook his head. She moved on to the next display area.

"Interesting piece," Alvin said.

Genevieve did a double take. He was staring at a stack of papers, plans her parents had made for future projects. The only actual anything that could be called a piece was a paperweight, but . . .

"My parents didn't make that," she said. "It's just there to keep the other things from blowing around when people walk past." Why had she used her own piece for that purpose?

Maybe because she didn't actually own another paperweight?

Alvin quickly lost interest and moved on. Lucas, on the other hand, eyed the little blown-glass, yellow-and-crystal castle carefully. He picked it up. "It's not mass produced."

She tried not to get flustered. Blushing wouldn't convince Alvin to buy anything. "No, it's by a local artist. One who hasn't done anything else for many years."

Lucas looked up from where he was just putting the paperweight down. He raised one sexy eyebrow. "That's a very . . . convenient statement," he said.

"Convenient? I'd say not," Alvin said. "I thought it was a Patchett original. I was just about to offer her a lot of money for it, more fool I. Let's just get right to what you meant to show me, all right?" And because he was getting grumpy, she showed him her parents' preliminary drawings of the very piece he had in his house.

"They're one of a kind," she said.

"I see," Alvin said with a satisfied smile. "This will make a nice complete display along with the sculpture in question. Yes. Yes, I'll take the drawings and have them framed and displayed," Alvin told her. "I'll write the check out right now."

"That's very gracious of you. But if you noticed, the invitation mentioned that our purpose tonight is to find sponsors for Angie's House. My parents would have loved to have been donors. So, if you're buying their work, is it safe to assume you're donating to the Angie's House Fund, too?" she asked with as earnest and commanding a smile as she could manage. Alvin looked less than sure about the donations, but she was still holding his drawings. "We're going to incorporate one of my parents' favorite paintings in the living room at Angie's House just as they would have wanted."

Lucas looked at her, his expression unreadable. Okay, she was donating her own personal copy of her parents' painting, she'd just decided. It would stir up interest in the open house that would follow. Besides, it was hers to give.

"You can't stop me donating my own property," she said.

For a minute Lucas looked taken aback. He probably thought she was being foolish, donating something worth so much money when she was living hand-to-mouth.

Then his eyes grew dark and . . . very sexy. He gave her a secretive smile. "That's a pretty sassy, confident statement, you know."

Yes, it was, wasn't it? Not like her at all, was it? Or not like her before Lucas started trusting her to do things she'd never done and demonstrating that she didn't have to back down in the face of adversity.

She lifted one shoulder in a seemingly casual shrug. "I have a . . . a very good confidence coach." And Lucas, her unintentional coach, let her make mistakes without criticism. He trusted her in a way no one ever had. He made her feel . . . powerful.

"Confidence coach?" Alvin said. "I never heard of anything so ridiculous, but you want to spend your money on coaches, I guess that's your business. I'm just glad you showed up with my sketches."

Alvin committed to a tidy sum; he walked away with a big smile, and Lucas and Genevieve exchanged a brief, private glance. "That was impressive," he said. She supposed he meant the amount Alvin had given, but she didn't have time to ask because just then another group of people entered the gallery.

They were led by a tall brunette.

"I didn't invite Rita," she said, her heart sinking. Rita might make a scene. Or wrap her arms around Lucas right here.

"I didn't invite her, either," Lucas added. "But I'm not totally surprised that she's here. Rita knows the art scene in great detail. She knows what's happening, she probably even saw the invitation, and there's no way she's going to miss out on an unusual showing like this one is. Furthermore, she knows we can't make a scene and ask her to leave without harming our cause. She's going to want to see all your parents' work."

"I just hope she doesn't out us," Genevieve said.

"There's a good chance she will if she doesn't get what she came for."

And Lucas would know. Judging from that first day at his office, he obviously knew Rita very well. Genevieve had a bad feeling that what Rita had come for was him.

Lucas watched as Rita roved the outer reaches of the gathering. She made eye contact with him several times, but he didn't appear to be her prey. Her attention seldom left Genevieve, and Rita watched as Gen interacted with the patrons.

For her part, Genevieve was nervous. No question of that. The fact that she refused to look at either him or Rita was proof of just how tense she was. On the other hand, her interactions with the other guests could not be faulted. She smiled brightly, even though once or twice he was close enough to hear someone mention her parents and the words *shopping addiction.* Once he even heard the word *cocaine.*

That was the only time she lost her smile. Lucas wanted to punch the man who had said it in his big fat nose. He even started to take a step closer to them. Then Genevieve looked up at him. Just that. She just looked, stark tension in her pretty green eyes, the tiniest shake of those russet curls, and he knew that she wouldn't thank him for his interference.

For a minute those take-care-of-business, make-things-work protective instincts he'd

176

honed for so long warred with the fact that he knew she wanted to handle this herself. She needed the confidence that taking care of things on her own would give her, but . . . hell, what the jerk had accused her of . . .

A small growl escaped him.

"You always were sexier than anything when you were being all protective." Rita's husky voice sounded at his side. "Go ahead. Do it. Looks like she needs some help."

He didn't even glance down at her. "She doesn't. She's stronger than you think." He remembered when she had dared him to tell her she couldn't donate her painting. "What are you here for, anyway, Rita? What's your goal?"

She laughed. "Hey, I'm just doing my job. Making sure that I know what's out there, what people are buying. Your little friend seems to be raking in some cash tonight. Or . . . no, she works for you, doesn't she? The little rich girl with such a taste for expensive things that she lost all her money. Well, looks like she's making some of that back tonight. Inferior product, though."

He glanced down at her. "It is, isn't it? But she's selling it. Lots of it. And making them fork over money for the charity, too. So, what does that tell you?"

Rita grimaced. "That I'd better watch my

back? If she ever decided to take up agenting, she might be able to sell her client's work even if it wasn't as good as that of my client's. You've just got to respect that, don't you?"

"I do respect that. And yes, I thought you might, too. You're not as harsh as you try to make yourself out to be."

Rita shrugged. "Sometimes I am. Sometimes a girl just needs to be a little angry, have a little pout. I knew all along that you weren't the type who played for keeps and for a brief time I forgot that. So, don't worry, Lucas. I'm not here for you. I'm just here to work. I think I'll go see if your assistant can talk me into buying anything."

"You don't buy. You sell."

"But I like art," Rita said, giving him a fake innocent look.

He clenched his hands into fists, wanting to tell her to leave Genevieve alone. His urge to control the situation and to protect Gen warred with the knowledge that stepping in to protect her would harm her. She was just beginning to feel her power. Having a man take it from her by acting as if he knew more than she did . . . ? Not happening, even if he actually did know Rita better than Genevieve did.

He glared daggers at Rita, but he said

nothing even though he needed to get back to chatting people up for the cause.

"You're looking very . . . involved with your project manager, Lucas. I'm sure I'm not the only one who's going to notice that and start wondering what's going on between you two if you don't tone things down a bit."

Were other people wondering what was going on? He didn't want people to think of Gen in terms of her relationship with him. She deserved better and she deserved her night in the spotlight. Solo. "It's not like that with Genevieve," he said.

"What is it like?"

It was like nothing he'd ever experienced before. "My relationship with Genevieve revolves around Angie's House and it's going to end very soon."

And the fact that his mind went dark at the thought of that impending farewell?

He'd just have to survive it. Because he had to. He was the worst kind of man for a woman like Genevieve, who needed to be free of overbearing people. She was just beginning to find herself, to unleash her spirit. She wanted her freedom, not him.

"So, how are you doing with the vultures?" Rita asked.

179

Startled at the sudden sound of the woman's voice behind her, Genevieve nearly dropped the clay figure she was holding. Carefully, she set it down next to some sketches. Up until a minute ago, she'd been busy with all the patrons who wanted a piece of never-before-released Patchett art. But she'd been totally aware of the striking beauty talking to Lucas. Right up until the minute Rita had left his side. Not that it was any of her business whether Rita and Lucas were together. Not her business at all. Even if a nice-size sliver of jealousy had slid through her when she realized how gorgeous they looked together.

"Vultures?" she asked as lightly as she could manage. "Is that what you call them?" Why *was* Rita talking to her?

Rita laughed. "Actually, I call them the people who pay my bills and my client's bills, but in this case, there was a slight resemblance. I'm not talking about the way they attacked your parents' stuff, either. Still, you seem to have withstood all the rude comments they were making."

Genevieve lifted one shoulder. "I'm still standing. But I'm not sure what you're here for. You don't want to buy my parents' work, do you?" She gestured to one of the sketches, one her mother had hated.

180

"Sorry. No, although I admire the way you manipulated the situation and got people to buy things they would normally have thrown in the trash."

Genevieve sucked in a breath, but she didn't deny the accusation of manipulation or the fact that the sketches were inferior. At least they were sticking to the subject of art and not discussing Lucas.

Although Rita's presence was a good reminder of how short-term Lucas's relationships were. It was also a reminder that Gen had, by losing herself in his kisses, fallen into yet another bad mistake with a man. And not just any man, not some jerk like Barry, but Lucas, a man she respected and . . . okay, she liked him. A lot. Too much. Far too much.

He would hate it if she fell for him.

She also felt at a disadvantage with Rita, a woman who not only knew as much about art as Gen did, but also knew how foolish it was to think about Lucas in terms of the future.

"Forgive me, but I'm afraid you have me at a disadvantage," she said, using the Lucas McDowell theory of bluffing one's way through a difficult, demeaning situation. "I'm not sure what you want from me, since the only time you and I met, you were giving me advice about Lucas. That's a conversation I'm not in the mood to continue."

Rita shrugged. "I can't blame you for that, but you needn't worry. I'm not interested in discussing Lucas or in trying to fight my way back into his good graces via you. Besides, I suspect that when things are over with Lucas, there's no going back. When he leaves, he's done." She gave Genevieve a pointed look, as if offering advice. "Anyway, he and I are both attack dogs. If we spent too much time together, we'd kill each other."

Instantly, Genevieve's hackles rose. Lucas had spent so much time learning how to keep his life on an even keel. That comment wasn't fair. "Lucas wouldn't attack. He has an iron will and he dislikes emotional scenes."

"Maybe, but when those people were giving you a hard time, he was straining at the leash, trying to keep from swooping in and decking someone."

"But he didn't."

"No," Rita conceded. "He probably knew that losing control would be very bad for the outcome of this affair. That's one man who understands good business practices inside and out."

It was much more complicated than that,

but Genevieve kept silent. Lucas's private reasons for his need for control weren't open for discussion.

"As to why I sought you out?" Rita shrugged. "I heard about this gathering, and I just wanted to see what all the buzz was about. Sorry about crashing your party." Although she didn't sound even vaguely repentant.

"By the way, who made the glass castle people keep eyeing? It's not your parents' style. Is the artist anyone I've heard of?"

Genevieve blinked. "I . . . no . . . I don't think so."

"Ah." Rita looked amused. "Was it you?"

"Yes." But Genevieve didn't want to talk about it, remembering how her parents had criticized the piece's childish garishness. Rita might not be nice, but her job was to know good art. So no matter how much Gen loved her embarrassing little castle, she wished she had left it at home. "The castle isn't art. I'm just using it to hold down the loose sketches, which might have blown around otherwise."

"Hmm . . . good idea. And you're right. It's not art, even though it's . . . interesting. I thought Harold Julette was going to lose an eyeball the way he had it pressed up to his face trying to see the detail inside. By the way, you could have gotten more money from Mr. Munion for the bird sketch. It's not collection quality, but he's a sucker for birds."

"Birds."

"Exactly. You can thank me next time you do business with him. Oh, well, gotta go. This little event was . . . instructional."

Gen was proud of what she had accomplished tonight, but she clearly wasn't truly independent yet. An independent woman would have simply left things alone. No reason to take the bait.

"What did you learn?" she asked Rita.

"That you have a decent eye for art and bad judgment where men are concerned. Stick with the art, but I'd prefer you stay out of my territory, please." She gave Genevieve a strained smile. And without another word, she left the room.

CHAPTER NINE

Lucas closed the door on the last volunteer. Then he turned to Genevieve, directing his full attention to her. And whenever Lucas directed his full attention to anything, he was a powerful force. Right now, he was looking at her like some fierce predator eyeing his prey. She gave him a tentative smile.

"I think that went well, don't you?" she asked. "Katy — one of the volunteers — told me that people were generous. She also told me that an inordinate number of the checks seemed to be scented with perfume. Hmm . . . you must have really charmed all those women, Lucas."

"*Were* there other women here tonight?" He advanced a step.

Genevieve melted. She desperately wanted to walk up to him and crush her mouth to his, but . . . that would be such a stupid move. Losing control around Lucas was getting to be a problem. Time was flying, and like so many women before her, she'd soon revert to her "no Lucas" status. A smart, independent woman wouldn't allow herself to even develop the craving, would she?

No. "I can't believe things turned out so well," she said, managing a bright, platonic smile, "but we gave out all our brochures, the food seemed to be a hit and I know that the men liked discussing sports with you and . . ."

"Genevieve?"

She looked up. As she did, Lucas walked up to her, slid his hands around her waist and pulled her to him, stopping her words with a kiss. "You are an incredibly amazing woman." He whispered the words against her lips. "I hope you know that."

What she knew was that he was simply high on the success of the evening, but with his body tight against hers and her lips tingling from his kiss, she felt pretty amazing.

"I don't want to be one of those annoying people who floats around gloating about their successes," she said.

He smiled against her lips. "Go ahead. Float. Gloat. You turned what had promised to be a less than stellar evening into something remarkable. Thank you."

"No. Thank you. From the first day you

186

hired me, I didn't think this would work, and I told you so repeatedly. If you hadn't pushed me, tonight wouldn't have happened. As it was, I had a perfect evening."

Lucas pulled back slightly. "Even Rita? She didn't call you out about your parents' art, but she seemed bent on testing you. Maybe I should have tossed her out instead of letting her confront you."

She shook her head. "No. I have to learn to deal with adversity."

"Did she insult you?" He scowled, his grip on her waist tightening slightly.

"I'm not sure. She agreed that my paperweight wasn't art, and she told me to stay out of her territory. It was the oddest thing." But Genevieve looked up to find Lucas smiling. "What?"

"Your paperweight *is* art, and she knows it. More people stopped to look at your glass castle than your parents' sketches and sculptures tonight. I know, because every time I looked up, a different person was holding it. As an expert in the field, Rita wouldn't have missed that. And if she's warning you away from her territory, then she considers you a threat. I suspect that if you wanted to, you could make a career change from project planner to agent. She knows that, too."

Genevieve felt as if her head was spinning. "What an evening."

"Exactly. Let's get you home before you lose your glass slipper, Cinderella."

But when the morning came, the problem that ensued was much greater than a missing glass slipper. Today was the day Genevieve was to begin interviews to find her eight residents. And one of last night's guests had shown up at the door with a complaint about the piece he'd bought.

There was chaos and confrontation at Angie's House. It was far too much like moving back in time, to the day when she'd finally realized that her parents would never love her. She wasn't what they'd hoped and planned for when they'd decided to have a baby.

Only this time the person complaining had decided that the Patchett sketch he'd bought was a fake.

Lucas was pacing, pacing, pacing, ready to grab that guy and throttle him. The man wanted his money back, interfering with the business of Angie's House and criticizing Genevieve. Lucas's hands doubled up into fists and his mind replayed times in his rough teenage years when he'd fought his way into and out of trouble. The difference between then and now was that then he'd been defending *himself.*

This was nothing like that, even though he was still a take-charge guy, a doer, a controller. *You can't just leave things like that,* he told himself. *She can't be two places at once and this has to be resolved.*

And if he stepped in and did his usual head-down, forge-ahead, take-charge, controlling attitude with Gen, if he insisted on wresting some of her power from her, what then?

She'd feel incompetent and assume he didn't trust her.

But if he did nothing and let her struggle with an impossible load, what then?

Catastrophe. She'd feel as if she'd failed if things fell apart.

Either way, she was going to feel awful. Both of them would lose no matter what he did or didn't do. And he couldn't leave things as they were. There was too much at stake.

Walking to where she was standing in front of the red-faced man, Lucas felt as if he were on his way to a funeral. His. Hers. The funeral of those few special moments they'd shared.

He stepped up beside her, got right between her and the red-faced guy yelling at her. What Lucas wanted to say was "Get away from Genevieve and shut up." But that would have completely stolen Gen's power, so what he ended up saying was "If you'll excuse me for just a minute, I need to speak to my project manager."

The man puffed up. "I'm not done with her."

"Neither am I. This will just take a minute."

Frowning and blustering, the man didn't say no. Lucas touched Genevieve's arm, ignoring the powerful heat that ripped through him every time they touched. "This won't take long," he assured her, shepherding her into the nearest doorway.

"I'm so sorry, Lucas," she said as soon as they were inside. "Don't worry. I'll fix this. I can do it. And . . . I apologize for the timing. I know that Mindy is due to arrive at any minute and . . ."

He placed two fingers over her lips, silencing her. Gently. Gently. "I know you can fix it, too," he told her. "I do know that. That's your part. All I need to know, all I want you to tell me is . . . what's my part?"

She blinked, suddenly silent, her beautiful green eyes huge as she stared at him. "I can't ask you to do my work. This is my area. I don't want to fall down on the job."

Lucas shook his head. "You won't. Gene-vieve, everyone needs help sometime. I hired *you* to be the project manager of Angie's House, because I can't do everything. I can't be in more than one place at a time. No one can. Not even an excellent project manager like you.

"My point is, asking for help when you need it doesn't make you less independent. It simply makes you smart. Someday you may have your own company or agency and you'll need to delegate. Today, you just have me, so, Genevieve, would you let me help you?"

He took his fingertips away from her mouth and she nodded slowly. "Yes. Yes, of course. I can handle Mr. Healey. He's just confused. Someone gave him some bad information and I can eventually set him straight, but . . . if you could meet Mindy, that would be so fantastic."

"Consider it done," he said, as he turned to go.

"Lucas?"

He looked back at her. "Thank you," she said.

"I'm sure that Mindy won't be a prob-lem," he assured her.

"No, not that. I know you'll make her feel like a queen. Thank you for trusting me."

191

"You earned it. Last night was proof that you've found your wings. You're ready to fly alone."

And in two weeks, that would happen. Angie's House was almost set to go. He'd received a call from France this morning. They already had meetings set up with the town authorities in order to begin work on his next store. In two weeks he and Genevieve would say their final farewells. Like every other woman he'd left behind, he'd probably never see her again.

The thought nearly stole his breath even though it wasn't anything he hadn't known from the very start.

He just hadn't known Genevieve when this whole thing began. Somehow, he had the sinking feeling that she would be much more difficult to forget than anyone he'd ever met or left.

Genevieve had taken the disgruntled customer to her office and finally managed to placate him. The man had barely left the room when Lucas walked in.

Immediately, his gaze went to the broken glass on the floor. Crystal and gold.

"What happened?" His voice was harsh. He looked as if he wanted to put his fist through a wall. Instead, he — very carefully

— leaned against the door frame. "Gene-vieve?"

She shook her head. "It's not what it looks like. Neither of us threw anything."

He gave a harsh laugh. "I was thinking more along the lines of a scuffle resulting in some broken glass."

"You think I would let it come to that?"

"Of course not, but I know from experi-ence that sometimes other people impose their will. Unanticipated things happen. What *did* happen? Please," he said, gentling his voice. "You look intact."

She couldn't help smiling. "Most people would say, you look fine, but yes I *am* intact. All in one piece. No harm done."

"I wouldn't say that." He glanced down at the shattered glass. "You lost something you loved."

Genevieve shrugged. "Mr. Healey got it into his head that the sketch he bought last night wasn't a true Patchett original."

"I hope you told him that you would know a Patchett original better than anyone."

Genevieve shuffled some papers on her desk. "He'd already heard something of my reputation. He wasn't exactly impressed with my credentials."

The pencil Lucas was holding snapped. "Really?" he said, putting it down carefully, exercising that superb control he had mastered. "Really?" Then he looked down at the broken glass and swore, temporarily losing control. "I assume you set him straight, worked everything out and sent him away happy."

For that comment alone she would have loved him. He was clearly angry, the evidence here pointed to a situation that had ended badly and yet he still believed that she'd brought everything to a satisfactory conclusion.

"I did. I bored him to death with a lesson on the Patchett signature complete with images, an excruciatingly long article my father had written and a video from experts who had studied the Patchett signature. Then I demonstrated the validity of his painting."

"Images, articles and a video?"

"My parents were fanatics about the brand. They made sure everything was well documented. I put it all together for them myself. Anyway, Mr. Healey left here a happy and slightly embarrassed man."

"Did he break your castle?"

"Not intentionally. He was banging on my desk and things were bouncing around. The castle fell off and hit the hardwood floor. It's all right."

Now he rose. "*You're* not all right. It was

a wonderful piece and it meant something to you."

"It was just a bauble."

"That you kept even though you made it when you were ten."

"My parents thought it was trash. I kept it to irritate them."

He slowly shook his head.

"You don't believe me?"

"You told me that you were a well-behaved, complacent child. Something doesn't fit."

He was right. She looked down at the sparkling broken bits of glass and said a sad internal goodbye to the piece she'd been moving from desk to desk for years. "Okay, maybe I'm a little sentimental. I was so excited the day that I made it. My parents worked in various mediums — they painted and sculpted but glass was their forte. I had hoped that finally I might do something that would make their eyes light up, but instead they said that I was simply playing at being an artist. It was obvious that they were disappointed."

"Maybe they didn't like the fact that your work might end up being more commercial than theirs."

Lucas's voice was cold, but the mere fact that he was trying to make her feel better brought a small smile to her face. "Nice try. Have you forgotten that I know art?"

"Not likely, but I'm taking a wild guess that you might not know the value of your own art, especially if your first efforts were shot down by pros like your parents. It would be tough to try again with critics like that. But I stand by my argument. I'm no art expert but I watched the guests at the party the other night. They were interested. If you hadn't kept insisting that it was a valueless paperweight that wasn't for sale, someone would have bought it."

She looked at him for a minute, just reveling in the sound of his voice and how indignant he was for her sake. "You're such a nice man, Lucas."

"If I were a nice man, I would have stopped the guy from breaking your treasure."

"No, you wouldn't. You know how much I need to handle things on my own."

He growled.

She smiled. "How did things go with Mindy? And . . . why are you back so soon? It must have been a short interview."

"It was. She called and when she found out that she was being interviewed by a man, she balked."

His tone betrayed nothing, but Genevieve's heart hurt for him. He was doing all he could to make a safe place, but . . .

"Will she let me interview her? Will she even be able to come live here if she fears men?"

"I spoke to the charity that recommended her. We're trying to get her into counseling and a more secluded safe place." His voice was harsh, raw.

"Lucas, you can't save everyone."

"I'm not trying to save them, just give them some happiness."

But she knew he lied. He would save them if he could.

"Genevieve . . ."

"Yes?"

"The call from Mindy made me think . . . perhaps we need to do more with security."

"We have an excellent alarm system that connects directly with the police station. This is a very quiet and historically safe neighborhood. The windows and doors have the best locks possible, the outside lighting is superb. What did you want to add?"

"Lessons."

She looked into his eyes. "I'm sorry. I don't understand."

"Self-defense lessons."

"That's so . . . fantastic! Why didn't I think of that?"

"I like to think that it's because you feel safe here."

"I do. But I can certainly understand why someone who has led a harsher life than I have might never feel safe. Anywhere." She immediately wished she hadn't said that. She wondered if Lucas was thinking of Angie.

He looked to the side. Now she *knew* he was thinking of Louisa, but when he turned to her, he surprised her. "Learning how to defend oneself can be a real confidence builder. It can make a person feel as if they can handle any situation."

"Then it's definitely something we should have here," she said softly.

"It's something any woman — or any man, for that matter — might need to know, don't you think?" he asked. And the way he gazed into her eyes told her that they had moved beyond Mindy.

"Every person should know how to defend themselves," she agreed. "Do you have any suggestions for instructors?" She reached for the pad of paper.

"For the school, yes." He scribbled down a number. "For you? I'll teach you."

He had moved closer to write the phone number down. Now they stood within inches of each other. "Why?" she asked.

"Because — from the comment you made — I assume you think that I lack confidence?"

"You have confidence. You could use more." He glanced down at the paperweight she had denigrated. "Besides, hate me for saying this if you must, but I'll worry less when I'm gone. I'll feel better leaving you if I know that you can take down the bad guys whenever you need to. Every independent woman should have a grab bag of techniques for dealing with those who want to steal her freedom from her."

"Why you?" She glanced down at the phone number.

"Because I want to. Because I owe you."

She frowned. "No. I work for you. You pay me."

"Not enough. That party the other night, your parents' display, the way you worked that room, all that you've done here, has been above and beyond what any other employee would have done."

"Maybe it's just because I'm inexperienced."

"Maybe it's just because you're good. Because you're you."

"Thank you."

"Will you feel . . . uncomfortable taking lessons from me?"

Oh, yeah. Because there was going to be touching. She was going to have to watch herself and not let her emotions get involved, not let him see how very much he affected her. "I wouldn't have it any other way."

He smiled, that gorgeous, achingly wonderful, suddenly boyish smile. How seldom he must have smiled as a boy. How grateful she was for the chance to see him smile now. And why was he smiling?

Because he likes to be in control and knowing that all the chess pieces are where he wants them to be makes him feel in control. If you're safe, that's one less piece he has to worry about.

"So we're good?" he asked.

"Almost. There's just one thing more." One more thing that would make him smile.

"Just tell me." He waited.

"About Barry . . ."

He glowered. "Has he called here? Or come by?"

"Lucas, no. Do you think I wouldn't have mentioned that?" Would she have mentioned it knowing how Lucas felt about men who took advantage of others? "I just meant . . . I've learned a lot working here and one of the things I've learned is that part of the reason Barry was able to take advantage of my situation was because I didn't feel comfortable managing my own money, so I let him handle things. I don't want to ever end up in that position, so I was wondering . . . before you leave, could you give me a few financial pointers? Things every responsible adult should know. I would like to feel in control of my finances. That is, if you wouldn't mind. I know you've got a lot to do before you go."

Okay, there was that smile she craved. "You shouldn't have even had to ask. Of course, you'll be a priority, Genevieve. I want you to walk out of here feeling secure in every way."

So did she. That way she'd be able to survive totally on her own and he'd find it easier to walk away without ever looking back. With no regrets.

Genevieve felt as if her throat was closing up. She felt close to tears. Her time with Lucas was winding down and soon he'd simply be a former employer, a man she knew for a few weeks.

No, he would always be much more than that, but she could never let him know that. If he knew that she was falling in love with him — and she was — he would regret having met her. He would hate himself for breaking her heart.

"Should we start tomorrow? That gives us a full two weeks."

"It will have to be enough time," he said. But she knew that two weeks with Lucas wasn't nearly enough time.

CHAPTER TEN

They had barely gotten started, Lucas thought the next day, and already these defense lessons were a strain. It brought him into close physical contact with Genevieve, and that was risky.

I should have hired a woman to teach her, he thought.

But he wanted to do it himself. Because he knew not only the right way to fight, but also the dirty way. He intended to show her all that he knew. When their time was up, she could walk away confident that she would be the one with the edge in an attack situation.

"Come at me as if you're going to flatten me," he ordered during this afternoon's training session. "Make me believe you're really capable of disarming me and taking me out of commission."

She did as he asked. She ran at him, but without any fire. "Genevieve, you know this is important."

"I do know. I *want* to do it. I need to know this stuff, but . . . what if the unthinkable happens and I actually hurt you in some way?"

"Gen, you're much smaller than me. You're a princess. I'm the big evil black knight. You're *not* going to hurt me."

"I see. I'm the weak one."

"You know that's not what I meant. I was talking about experience and intent. You're too nice."

"I can be mean." She bared her teeth. And had him laughing.

"Gen, you're supposed to take me down with your skill, not make me collapse because I'm laughing so hard."

"I just feel so uncomfortable trying to hit someone I . . . I like."

That word — *like* — nearly brought him to his knees. He didn't want her to like him.

"Oh, look at that frown. Now I've really made you mad. Here you are trying to help me and I'm giving you a half-baked effort."

"No, you're fine, Genevieve. Really." And her liking him was good. It was smart. Better than love, which was so . . . wrong. He couldn't selfishly want her to love him. She'd just discovered her independence, and she reveled in it. She wanted to be alone. How could he even consider robbing her of that?

"Maybe mean isn't a good goal for you," he conceded. "Try for confident. That's good enough. If you look like you're confident, that's half the battle of keeping the bad guys at bay."

"Confident. Hmm . . ."

"Like when Mr. Healey accused you of cheating him and you showed him slides and videos."

She wrinkled her nose, but she instantly demonstrated confidence.

He laughed. "Great. Now stop thinking of me as Mr. Healey and pretend I'm a bad guy who could hurt you."

She didn't look suitably upset. A little fear was good going into a fight. It produced the necessary adrenaline.

"I *have* hurt people," he said. "More than you know."

He was hoping to shock her with news he didn't usually share, and he apparently had. But she still didn't look angry or afraid. "I know that had to have been a terrible time in your life," she said, her voice radiating sadness and concern.

And suddenly the tables had been turned. He was losing his focus. *Focus,* he ordered himself. Gen needed to know how to do these things.

"Okay, let me show you something," he said and he showed her a move designed to trip him up and give her the upper hand. "Now, charge me."

She charged, without much spirit but with more than the first time. When she planted her palms on his body, her momentum carried her forward still more. Her chest met his and they slowly tumbled backward in a rolling motion that landed them both on the ground, limbs tangled. Lucas was in a half-sitting position with Genevieve's knee within kissing distance of his mouth.

"Good try," he said.

Some muffled laughter sounded from somewhere beneath his elbow. "You have got to be kidding me," Genevieve said. "That didn't even rate."

"You made the attempt."

"You can't mean to tell me that this was how it was supposed to work out."

"No, I can't. This isn't the best way to take down a man." Although he was both down and a man.

"I hope I can get this right," she said, her voice turning a bit forlorn. By now she had disentangled herself, he was flat on his back and she was kneeling above him, her palm resting on his chest. "I was never particularly skilled at the physical arts."

Oh, how he wished she had not said that. It made him think of Gen in a bed with a breeze blowing in and moonlight on her body, his lips on her . . . softness. Everywhere.

Stop, he ordered himself. "I'm positive that you'll do just fine." Somehow he managed to rasp out the words. "You just need a little practice." And then, because she was so close and he was so very tempted, he reached up and drew her down to him, nuzzling her mouth.

A low, sweet moan escaped her. She leaned closer, plunged her fingers into his hair and returned his kiss. She was soft, warm, her body pressed to his. She kissed him again and again.

Desire speared through him. He wanted to fight it. He knew that someone like Gen didn't do this kind of thing every day. Maybe never. And he didn't want her to think he was taking advantage of the situation. Especially since he was the one who had suggested the lessons.

"Gen?"

"Mmm?"

"You should —" He groaned. "You should try to knock me down again. I'm afraid I'm not the best teacher in the world."

She froze. She looked down at him. "You're a great teacher, but . . . I think we'd better try again tomorrow," she said.

"Yes." Maybe by tomorrow, he would be more in control.

"I'll study. I'll try harder."

"I won't kiss you next time," he said. "Just in case you're worried that I might take advantage of the situation."

She gave him a slow, sad smile. "Lucas, I'm sure you must know that I like kissing you." And as if to demonstrate, she brushed her sweet, berry lips against his. Right then. Right there. "I just don't want to like it."

It was a most unusual ending to a lesson, he thought later as he tried to think of ways to improve his presentation. What should he have done better?

Kissed her more. It was the wrong answer. And he was probably the wrong teacher for her. But he was determined to somehow end this right. If he gave her any reason to regret having known him, he'd have nightmares for life. And no amount of Angie's Houses could cure that.

Genevieve was on her fourth interview and it was proving to be an emotional experience. She was glad that Lucas was letting her handle this part of the project, because she wasn't sure he could stand the parade of sad women who passed through the doors, or the fact that when she told them who was responsible for their good fortune, they wanted to kiss Lucas's feet.

And they hadn't even met him!

He would have felt uncomfortable with all that gratitude, undeserving. Worse, he would have been saddened by the fact that she couldn't even interview all the candidates yet. There simply wasn't room at Angie's House. At least not yet. Or at least not this one.

And unless this one was a success there might not be another one. Now that she was at this stage, she realized how perfect everything had to be.

She was thinking about that when she passed Lucas on the stairs, her arm brushing his.

As if it had been rehearsed, they both looked up, gray eyes staring into green. He slid his palm around her waist; she slipped an arm around his neck. They shared one hot, hot kiss. One very fast kiss. Then they moved on.

"I'll see you in the gym," he said.

"Three o'clock," she agreed. Her body began to ache just thinking about it. Not that anything was happening. Since that first day, they had stuck to the plan. He instructed and demonstrated. She attacked and carried out his instructions. They barely even spoke beyond his commands.

She was getting good. But the lessons were total torture. She knew he felt the same. Neither of them wanted to end up in an embrace that threatened to get out of hand again.

So, even though they kissed at times like this, the encounter was always brief, often in a public place so that they had to end things soon. Sometimes, like on the stairs, they had to pay attention or lose their balance.

She couldn't wait for the two weeks and the torture to end. She couldn't bear to think of it ending. Their fate had been preordained, back when Lucas was a boy. Back when she was growing up. Who they had once been, who they were now, their limitations, their futures had all been set by unpleasant circumstances and now they were two planets whose paths had, temporarily, crossed but would soon move on their separate ways.

The smart thing to do would be to simply ride out the next two weeks, do her job, have a very simple open house for the sponsors and the public and then say goodbye.

Very dignified. Nothing messy or risky. That was the smart thing. The reality was something different.

One morning she gathered her new recruits, the soon to be new residents of Angie's House. She picked up Della, the woman she'd hired to be the director. "Ladies, we have a challenge," she said. "In less than a week, Angie's House will open its doors and let the world inside for one day only. You don't have to attend if you don't want to. This will be your home, but we don't want you to ever feel uncomfortable or overwhelmed. So, it will be your choice. There will be members of the press, some local dignitaries, some sponsors, some neighbors, myself, Lucas and any of you who want to be there. So, give it some thought."

That had been her only intent, to give fair warning and offer them a choice.

Then things changed.

"If this is our home, and this is a party, can we help plan it?" one woman asked.

"Yes, can we do that? That would be so fantastic! I've never lived in a place where I had the room or the money to even have a party," another woman said.

"And you said Lucas would be there? He's so handsome. I've seen him," the first

211

woman volunteered.

"We'll get to mingle with him. Won't we?"

Suddenly all nine faces were turned toward Genevieve. "You can talk to him as much as you like," she said.

The women exchanged looks. Then one of them turned back to Genevieve. "You know, Lucas and you . . . I feel as if you're saving my life. Seriously. Saving it. If I'd had to stay where I am, I'm not sure I would have made it through another year."

"You're saving my sanity," another woman said. "Lucas and you. I wish I had the words to tell him that, but I'm not real good with words. I'm not sure I could even tell him what I'm telling you now if I had to say it to his face. Do you think . . . could *you* tell him how much this means to me?"

"I'll tell him," Genevieve said, her voice so thick with tears that it nearly came out in a whisper. Lucas had spent his life so alone, always feeling that he was damaging some woman. Had any woman ever said words like this to him? "I'll tell him," she repeated. "And maybe also . . ."

The women leaned forward in their seats.

"I have an idea," Genevieve said. And that was when things got really messy and crazy and veered away from her idea of the tasteful open house that she had promised Lucas.

Genevieve sat in her office, staring at her desk. A little glass castle paperweight sat there, the successor to the broken one. Only this one was from a store. It was very delicate, very pretty, rather expensive.

She hated it.

"Stop that," she told herself. "You don't hate it. You just . . ."

Hate everything right now. Which was totally unlike her. And totally because she didn't want to leave Lucas. Today was going to be her last self-defense lesson. She'd read all the financial information Lucas had given her. Right now she was a lean, mean self-defense machine and she could do her taxes or manage her retirement fund with her eyes closed. Someday she was going to be really happy for those things. But today?

"I miss him already." She was doing her best not to send him longing looks or get teary-eyed in his presence or indulge in too many kisses. In fact, they hadn't touched outside of class since that incident on the stairs.

Lucas was apparently pulling away, backing off, doing what he always did with women.

Like Rita.

For a moment, Genevieve felt a trickle of sympathy for the woman, even though Rita had called her several times in the past week or two to remind her that once Lucas was gone and she no longer had a job at Angie's House, she was not to think of taking up a job selling art the way she had at that party. She wasn't to poach on Rita's territory.

Lucas had been amused. "She must really think you're good if she's going to this much trouble to make sure you don't compete with her."

"Maybe she just wants to talk to you but she doesn't want to say so. You know, the way girls do."

"Not really."

She turned to look at him. And realized he was being truthful. He'd missed out on all the silly things young girls do to get the attention of guys, because at that time he'd been fighting just to stay alive.

"It's just a dumb thing. You call a man and if he answers, you pretend you were calling to talk to someone else at the house, but in reality you try to keep him on the line talking to you."

He looked flabbergasted. "So . . . you did that?"

She blushed and ducked her head, her hair swinging forward. "I didn't have a lot

214

of time for girl stuff, but Rita probably did. She probably called just to talk to you."

"Maybe, but when I spoke with her, she mostly wanted to talk about you. She wanted to know if you were making any more glasswork."

"Why?"

He smiled. "Because it's pretty and it's very you. Unique." He dropped a kiss on the top of her head. "Think about it."

She thought about it now. And dismissed it. She wasn't interested in talking to Rita. Rita would just say things about Lucas that she already knew. Tough stuff. Painful stuff.

Later when she was working with the ladies on the plans for the open house, one of them looked at her. "What are you going to do for Lucas?" the woman asked. "You know, like a 'going away' card. He'll be leaving and you won't. At least not right away."

Genevieve wondered if she could manage a card or think of the right things to say.

As for staying here, she loved this place, but she really did have to think about getting a job. She didn't want to be here when Lucas returned from his trip. It wouldn't be fair to him. She needed to get out.

But what could she do? Where could she go?

She looked at the want ads, spoke to

Teresa. Finally she picked up the phone and took a deep breath. "Hello, Rita," she said.

And then, five minutes later . . . "I want to be able to tell him that I'm leaving," she continued. "Make a clean break. No loose ends. Something he can count on. Nothing messy. Totally controlled. Just the way he likes it, you know?"

"I know, babe," Rita said. "Come over. We'll talk. I'll get you out of there. And I'll help you."

CHAPTER ELEVEN

"I don't want to have another lesson, and you don't need one, anyway," Lucas said. "This is the last day. Tonight's the open house and tomorrow I fly to France. You'll be here next week and the week after?"

"Yes. By then Della will be totally in control of the situation. She's almost there now. And I have some . . . possibilities for afterward." She didn't know why she said that when everything was still very much up in the air and she had no details. But he liked things in their place and she didn't want him to worry about her.

He was studying her, with those intense dark eyes. She knew he wouldn't ask what the possibilities were. Lucas had been her biggest cheerleader on her path to independence. He wouldn't pry.

"So, no lesson?" She got up to leave.

He reached out and took her hand. "I was hoping you could go somewhere with me today."

"Of course. Where?"

"I'm not big on surprises, but I think I'd like this to be a surprise. I want your first impression. We'll be gone most of the day. I'll let Della know in case she runs into any problems with any last-minute open house preparations."

"Most of the day?"

"It's pretty far away. Will you mind?"

Mind snatching every last drop of her time with Lucas? "I won't mind," she said. "The preparations are in order. There's not much left to do."

He touched her arm, gently, and she walked with him to the car, his skin brushing hers. The thought of spending the day with Lucas filled her with longing, because she loved him. It filled her with fear, because she was afraid she still might slip and let him know. And she was also experiencing a sense of impending doom. He didn't like surprises. That could be a problem tonight.

Lucas didn't know why he was doing this. Why had he bought this place? Why was he taking Genevieve there on a day when she probably had a ton of things she wanted to do and was just too polite to say so?

They had been driving for an hour, making small talk about Angie's House, about his business, about France. He noticed that whenever he tried to bring the topic back to her and what she would be doing, she gave some vague sprightly answer, then turned the conversation to him.

She didn't want him to know anything of her future. He had to respect that. She'd told him so many times that she needed her independence and would not want to rely on a man. Intruding, trying to pry or push himself into her plans would be wrong.

Not knowing what the future held for her was making him crazy. That was half the reason for this outing. He was going slowly insane thinking about leaving Genevieve and he had to have a day of just . . .

"I bought it last week," he said, shunting his thoughts aside and indicating the long, low house that stretched over the land and nearly kissed the lake behind it. "Fox Lake is a little far away from the city, but I thought . . . this might be the next Angie's House. I know you've been worried about the women who are on the waiting list. I didn't want to wait to see how the first one works out. If there's a need, I'd like to try to fill it. What do you think?"

They exited the car and she walked down the slope of the land to the house and then to the lake beyond. "I think it's perfectly beautiful here. The next group of women are going to be very lucky. You certainly know what women want."

He laughed. She knew that that wasn't so. In fact, he realized now that he'd been holding his breath, hoping she liked the place. This could have gone so wrong. Not everyone liked water or long commutes that ended far away from a true city.

"Come inside," he said, taking her hand. "I'd like your expert opinion."

She followed him through the house. "I love the window seats!" she said, dropping her purse and running to sit on the cushioned seat overlooking the lake. "And the huge sunroom that looks out on the gardens. The double fireplace and the deck, the pier, the water. Everything. I love it all." Her eyes were bright, her smile was electric. She was practically bouncing with excitement. "Lucas, this is so perfect. The next group of ladies are going to love this so much."

"Even that painting over the fireplace?"

She looked up. He held his breath. It had taken him some time to locate it, but he'd finally found the sister painting to the one she had donated to Angie's House.

"You found it." She barely breathed the words. "I love it. I love all of it. How did you find anything so perfect?"

"Maybe I just asked myself 'What would Genevieve like?' Your enthusiasm was my incentive. You make things easy. You've made these past few weeks easy."

"It's my job," she said, blushing in that pretty way she had. "Anyone would be excited about this place."

He shook his head. "I don't think so. You're unique. You're going to be difficult to forget." He wanted to tell her that he wouldn't ever forget her, but if he took it that far, she might know how he really felt. His Gen was an intuitive lady. And he didn't want her to feel sorry that she couldn't love him. Most of all he didn't want her to feel sorry *for* him.

It was time to lighten things up. If this was their last day together, he didn't want to spend it regretting what he couldn't have. She was here. Now. His for a few hours. It would have to be enough.

A hundred years of Genevieve would never be enough. But he was a man who was used to living on less than he wanted.

"Do you swim?" he asked.

"A little, but . . ." She looked down at the black slacks and royal-blue blouse she was wearing.

"That's not a problem. First room on the

right. There's a suit and a cover-up. Della raided your closet." He hoped she wouldn't mind that he had presumed to leave some things here for her. "I wasn't sure if you'd be able to come," he said. "I wanted to be ready."

Genevieve disappeared into the bedroom. He heard a shriek. "Did you tell Della what to pick?"

Uh-oh. "I've never looked in your closet. Is it something you don't like?"

"Well . . ." She walked out of the room. The plum-colored suit was cut in a deep V and had scooped out sides. It fit her curves to perfection. A low-slung lavender sarong rode her pretty hips. "This was one that Teresa talked me into buying once and I've never worn it. It always seemed too revealing for someone like me."

The suit *was* revealing, but it also looked as if the designer had had Gen in mind when he made it. "You're beautiful. You'll be the belle of the lake." But with her fair skin, he wouldn't want to keep her out long.

Ten minutes later, they were cruising the lake with the wind in their faces. Genevieve's coppery curls blew back from her face and whipped around her pretty cheeks. "This is wonderful!" she yelled. "I've never spent much time in a boat."

"Then you should spend more. Take some time to enjoy the wind in your hair." But there wouldn't be time for more.

When they returned to shore, she challenged him to a race, rushing into the water and swimming to a pier not far from the shore. She turned and waited as he pulled up beside her. "Did you let me win?" she asked, playfully punching him on the arm.

"Gen, do I look stupid? What man would let you win, knowing that you would probably punch him on the arm? Anyway, you cheated. You dove in without telling me that we were racing."

"I cheated? Me. I never cheat." Then she blushed prettily, because of course, she had. "Well, maybe I did this time. I was overexcited."

He closed his eyes. He didn't want to think of Genevieve overexcited.

"Lucas?"

He opened his eyes.

She smiled at him. "Fair warning. I'll race you."

Then, because she was obviously trying to be so darn fair, she let him start first. He won. Then she won the next one, shrieking with delight.

Finally, they fell on the shore beneath the shade of some trees and let the breeze dry them off. She lay back on her elbows and smiled up at him as he rose to his feet and held out his hand, pulling her up beside him.

"I like your house, Lucas," she said.

"Thank you. But it's not really mine. I'm donating it."

She gave a tight nod. "Oh, yes, you live in hotels. I guess that makes sense given your work schedule and all the traveling you do."

It made sense, but for today he wished he had a home. Here. With Genevieve.

"Time to go?" she asked as he led her back toward the house.

"Almost. I wanted to show you the orchard. In the spring this will be a mass of flowers. The former owner told me that he used to have weddings and picnics in among the trees. I thought the women might like that. And away from the city, they could have pets if they wanted them."

Genevieve was facing away from him, but when she turned back around, her eyes were misty with unshed tears. "You think of everything, don't you?" she asked. "You live in a hotel but you try to make sure that the women of Angie's House have orchards and blossoms and puppies."

"Don't cry, Gen. It's an extremely nice hotel. All of them are."

She laughed then. "I'm sure they're all the best hotels imaginable. I don't know why I'm being so maudlin. I just . . . this is so beautiful, Lucas. Thank you very much for sharing it with me."

And that was when he broke. "Gen, don't be polite. Don't share platitudes with me. I'm going, Gen. Tomorrow."

"I know. I'm going to miss you like crazy. And . . ."

"And . . ."

She moaned. "And if I don't do this, I'm going to regret it forever." She walked into his arms then, she lifted her lips, rose on her pretty pink toes, and his quiet little artist kissed him like he'd never been kissed before.

"Gen," he groaned. "Don't do this to me." But even as he said the words, he had gathered a fistful of her beautiful hair and urged her closer to him. They were knee to knee now, hip to hip, and he was going slowly, maddeningly insane.

"I'll stop," she said. "I will."

But she didn't. She swept her hand down his body, making his breath catch, making him crazy for her.

"Don't stop. Kiss me again." And thank the stars and the apple trees, she kissed him. Slowly. Wonderfully. She made him her own.

Time seemed to stand still. For this woman, time would. She was a miracle and had been a miracle since the moment he'd met her.

"Lucas?" she whispered.

"Tell me." He curved his palm around her jaw, urging her to look at him.

"Don't make me ask," she pleaded, and those big green eyes slayed him. He could barely think straight. He wanted her like parched earth wants water. He had to have her, but . . .

"You might feel differently tomorrow. I don't want to hurt you," he whispered.

She gave him one solitary kiss, one kiss that wasn't nearly enough. "You can't protect me, Lucas. I'm my own woman. And tomorrow is tomorrow. Today is all we can have."

He led her to the sunroom and there on the deep carpeting of the empty room, with blue sky overhead and the chirping of birds outside, he undressed her. He shed his suit and joined her there.

Then, he kissed her . . . deeply. He loved her . . . the way he'd wanted to for ages. And when she came to him, she did so with clear eyes, as solemn as a whisper.

"I'm never going to forget you, Lucas McDowell. You changed my life." She placed her palms on his chest and rose to meet him. "Love me today."

He would love her forever, but she would never know. "Any time you ever need anything, Gen. Any help, any anything. Whenever. Wherever. You let me know," he said.

"I will," she whispered. "I will. I need you now." And then she was his. Gen gave him today. And all that she was. The sun had never shone so brightly. Nor would it ever again.

As they drove home, heading toward the end of their time together, he knew that she would never call him, never let him know anything, despite what she had said. His Gen was too much her own woman.

And none of his.

Except in the secret recesses of his heart.

Hours later, Genevieve stood in the foyer of Angie's House and tried not to think about the perfection and the wonder of this afternoon or the staggering pain she felt when it had ended. Right now, she had a job to do.

The Angie's House open house was to be the culminating event of everything she'd done since she'd arrived here. It was the big show, the time when the project could shine for the masses, get some much deserved press and make an impression that could impact all future projects.

It was important that everything should go just right and that there should be no mishaps. So Genevieve was happy that she had prepared everything well in advance, scripted the entire evening and double-checked every detail with Della.

Nothing could go wrong.

Except for the unscripted part, the surprise part, the part she was petrified was going to embarrass Lucas. He'd never been a man who craved the spotlight. He'd told her just today that he wasn't fond of surprises.

And yet . . .

He'd surprised her today. *He kissed me. He did more, and he gave me a day I would never forget.*

But now she was lost. Wanting to be in Lucas's arms had been torture. Actually being in is arms, having him make love to her and knowing that her time with him was over . . . Genevieve's heart was slowly shattering. Her mind was like a sieve. Nothing was sticking. Nothing mattered.

Except it did. This was *his* night, and in pain or not, she had better get her act together. She would never forgive herself if she messed up any of tonight.

"Ready?" Lucas asked, as they opened the

door and let their guests in.

"Yes. This is finally it, the day we've worked for."

"Then let's do it." He brushed his knuckle across her cheek. "Let's officially open the first Angie's House."

She nodded. "Let's light a birthday candle for Angie's daughter."

At that, he held her gaze for a moment. And then they were torn apart by duty, the press, their guests.

Lucas stepped up to a podium they had placed there. A towering, impressive figure in formal black and white, he held the visitors' rapt attention as he gave a brief all-business, all-Lucas intro to the concept of Angie's House. Then Della and the new residents — all of them had opted to participate — came out and greeted everyone, including their new neighbors. They beamed when they were greeted by a round of applause. It was probably the first time some of them had ever received this kind of adulation.

"I feel like a star," one woman told Genevieve.

"You *are* a star, Lucy," Genevieve whispered. She felt tears come to her eyes when Lucy gave her a hug and when she looked up, she found Lucas looking directly at her.

He looked proud, intense, the best part of her world. He looked like . . . everything she wanted and could never have. Somehow she managed to smile back and keep her head high.

"And here's the woman who made so much of Angie's House happen," Lucas said, catching Genevieve by surprise. She stood and smiled at the crowd, acknowledging the applause.

When all the introductions were over, there were thank-yous to all the sponsors. There was food and talk, mingling and videos and tours of the house.

Then Genevieve gave a nod to the women of Angie's House. "We have one more item on the agenda tonight. Our new residents have something they'd like to share with all of you, but particularly with Lucas, the man who envisioned a place where women who had faced tough times could be given safety, encouragement, nurturing and a home where they could shine and receive a new life.

"These eight women you met earlier are very incredible ladies and they — the women of Angie's House — wanted to do something special to thank Lucas, something personal and unique. With that in mind, they've — no, *we've* — prepared

230

something to tell him what Angie's House has meant to those of us who have been blessed to call this special place our home. So . . . without further ado, if you'll please turn your attention to the windows, we'd like to present an Angie's House art show."

As she finished the speech, she stared into Lucas's eyes. And hoped he wouldn't be embarrassed by all the attention.

"Ladies," she said softly. "This is your home, and you're the hostesses. It's your show now."

At that, each of the women moved to the windows. Genevieve nodded to one of the servers, who began to raise the heavy curtains that had been concealing the eight canvasses that hung beneath. Each one had been created according to the painter's abilities. There were paintings of flowers in bright splashy reds and blues and yellows; there were more sophisticated and sedate birds and animals; there were mirror mosaics and collages. There was, in fact, only one common thread running through each work of art: a message printed or painted or otherwise meshed into the image. A message to Lucas.

The first woman stepped forward and smiled shyly. "Lucas gave me the chance to get my life back," she read.

"Lucas gave me hope when I had none," the next woman said.

"Lucas made me feel that I would smile again."

On and on, each one different, each one a tribute from the heart. As the crowd turned their attention from one woman to the next, the budding artist read her message. Some of them blushed, some of them mumbled shyly, but no one faltered and all of them read directly from the heart while looking at Lucas. Every one of them smiled at him, though that hadn't been a part of the plan. Finally, there were no more.

Or so it seemed.

Genevieve looked down. She held her breath, closed her mind to the public manner she was doing this. Then, opening the small bag she was carrying that night, she removed the only thing inside, a miniature replica of Angie's House, all in blown glass.

Placing it on her palm, she rose and walked up to Lucas. Through tear-misted eyes, she looked at him. "As the first resident of Angie's House, Lucas, you gave me a home. You turned my life around and sent me in a new direction. You gave me back my art."

She held out the small bit of glass and he took it from her, their fingers touching. For what seemed like forever, he held her gaze, his own fierce and intense. The room disappeared and all she saw was Lucas.

For one second, he leaned toward her. She leaned to meet him.

Then a whisper sounded behind them and both of them froze.

"Thank you, Genevieve. You've been a tremendous gift and I'll never forget you. Or this. I'll treasure it always," he said softly, formally, as he held up the tiny glass house for everyone to see.

He dropped a light kiss on her cheek. The guests broke into applause. This was, Genevieve realized, probably the last time she and Lucas would ever touch. Her cheek burned, her heart ached. Somehow she smiled as if nothing was wrong.

Soon after that, the guests all faded away. The women of Angie's House made their way to bed. All that remained were Lucas and Genevieve.

She didn't know how she would ever do this without breaking down. Words seemed impossible. *Movement* seemed impossible.

Yet, somehow she managed to walk with him to the door and out into the night. Just as if this were an ordinary parting.

Together they stood there. The wind lifted her curls. He brushed them back from her face. "Have a wonderful life, Gen," he finally said. "And don't forget to lock your doors."

She somehow smiled. "I won't. I have six locks, you know," she said.

He returned the smile. "Good night, Gen."

"Goodbye, Lucas." *Goodbye forever.*

And as he got into his car and drove off, her heart followed him . . . until the night took him away.

CHAPTER TWELVE

Six weeks. It had been six weeks since he'd awakened to find Genevieve gone, Lucas thought. He'd wrapped up matters at Angie's House within two days and flown to France. He'd been there and traveling around Europe ever since.

Now, he was supposed to be leaving for Japan.

He glanced down at the bit of glass he was holding, pressing the cell phone to his ear. "So . . . Genevieve's creating a stir with her work. That's wonderful," he told Rita. "I'm not surprised and I'm overjoyed that she's so successful." But he didn't ask Rita to send his good wishes. He didn't intend to intrude in Gen's life in any way.

"Not half as happy as I am," Rita said. "I'm over the moon that I have the job of representing the new up-and-coming It girl of the art world. We're starting out small, she's still a budding phenomenon, but everywhere she shows up, people go crazy, they act like kids when they see one of her miniature castles or free-form pieces. The fact that she's so likable just seems to fuel people's desire to have a piece of her, even if it's only a piece of her glass. I've seen men follow Genevieve around like lost puppies eager for attention, and Della says that Gen has become a favorite visitor at Angie's House, giving lessons to the women there."

"She was always amazing," he said. *And she's got her life exactly the way she wants it, doing what she wants to do. She's her own woman, free and independent, unfettered by anyone or any man. Finally, she's getting the recognition she should have had years ago if her parents had been the kind of parents they should have been. So, don't think of doing anything to mess with all of that,* he told himself.

He wouldn't. He'd never do anything that would hurt her. Never. But he had to see her just one more time. Rita might have lost sight of the reason for this phone call, but he had not. Just a few minutes ago, when he'd first picked up the phone, she had told him that despite everything, something wasn't right with Gen. Genevieve was fretting about something. Rita didn't know what it was. He suspected that she had called, thinking that he could work some magic and get Genevieve to crank up the production. Her greatest fear seemed to be that if Genevieve was upset, she might not meet the deadlines for a show Rita had arranged.

Lucas growled. He didn't know what was wrong with Genevieve, either, and he didn't give a damn about her production. But when he'd told Rita that, she'd clammed up and — darn the distance that separated them — she'd gotten so caught up in her need to communicate her enthusiasm for her own good fortune at representing Genevieve he hadn't been able to glean any more information from her. She'd gotten very testy when he'd suggested that she stop pressing Genevieve to increase her work hours.

Now, he sat looking at the glass he held in his hand. Something was wrong with Genevieve, he thought, and everyone seemed more interested in her work than in the woman herself. That wasn't right. And something else wasn't right, either.

It ended all wrong, McDowell. You didn't tell her the important stuff, things she needed to know. That wasn't right. At all. Fix it. Now.

Oh, yes, he knew that his motivations weren't entirely unselfish, if he was honest.

He couldn't very well criticize Rita when he would kill just for the chance to look at Genevieve one more time. But she mustn't know how much he cared, how much he missed her, that he was dying here without her. Because what he had to tell her, the thing she needed to know, was far more important than he was.

If she was in any way unhappy, then . . .

He looked at the glass again, turning it over in his palm. It gleamed and winked. "I can give you one last gift, Gen," he whispered. "I've discovered a secret that might make you feel a little bit better."

And he wasn't letting anyone stop him from doing that. He called the people in Japan and told them he wouldn't be coming. He'd fix all of that later. When he cared again.

Right now the only thing he cared about was getting to Genevieve.

Genevieve was holding her weekly art class at Angie's House. It was her favorite time of the week. Anyone who wanted to could show up and do anything their creative energies told them to do. And they came. They drew. They painted. Almost none of the work was the kind of stuff that Rita would look at twice.

But to Genevieve, it was all beautiful. Because there was hope and love in every piece of work produced here. Here was the one place where she could just be Genevieve and not a commercial commodity. There was only one problem, one overwhelmingly big problem. Every time she came here . . . the place resonated with memories of Lucas. She could barely walk through the halls without remembering his rare, beautiful laughter; she could never go into the bedroom where she had messed up the paint job and he had kissed her for the first time. And when she left Angie's House . . . tears threatened every single time.

A part of her wanted to stop going, because the experience was so dreadfully painful. But she couldn't. These women were her friends. She couldn't help wondering how Lucas was doing. She sometimes thought of asking Rita, because Rita seemed to know everything, but Rita had never had any qualms about discussing Lucas's relationships with women, and Gen wasn't sure she could handle hearing who Lucas was spending his time with now.

So, she dove into her lessons with the women and tried to block out the ghosts of the days she'd spent here with Lucas. She would keep doing this until her body and brain gave out, until the pain from her loss of Lucas grew dimmer or until she broke from the ache of wanting him.

"Lucy, that's a wonderful hat you've crocheted," Genevieve said, looking at the wobbly orange thing Lucy was sticking her hook into. Lucy was into crafts. She had no skill, but she loved the process, and Gen loved her attitude. She knew that Lucy had suffered a lot in her life and still managed to smile. It gave Genevieve hope for her own future self. "It's very —"

"Big," Lucy said, plopping the hat on her head where it promptly drooped down over her eyebrows. "But you know what? I like it, anyway, and . . . Hello, Lucas."

Hello, Lucas? The air stalled in Genevieve's lungs, her body felt tight, her eyes felt . . .

Don't cry, don't cry, don't you dare cry, she ordered herself as she slowly turned around. "Lucas?" Somehow she got the word out past the lump in her throat, even though her voice came out a bit thin and high-pitched.

He pinned her with his gaze, his eyes fierce and hot and . . . something else she didn't quite recognize. No, she did. He was upset about something. "I heard that you

240

were giving lessons here."

"Yes. I know I was supposed to be gone from here weeks ago. You don't mind that I'm doing this, do you?"

He and Lucy exchanged a look. He greeted the woman. "She wants to know if it's okay if she volunteers her time."

Lucy giggled. "I know. She's amazing, isn't she? She even tells us that the stuff we make is beautiful."

"Genevieve always had a kind heart and a good eye," he said. "Nice hat."

Lucy smiled. But she took one more look at Lucas and the expression in his eyes and said, "I think . . . I should go check out what's for dinner tonight."

For the first time, Genevieve panicked around Lucas. She had barely been able to keep from crying, she could hardly speak. The risk of him seeing what had to be written in her eyes was too great.

"I'm sure it's something good," she said, pulling on Lucy's arm to hold her still.

Lucy looked down at Gen. "Gen, you're always so brave and sure of yourself. Why are you holding my arm? You know Lucas is our friend and he isn't going to bite you. I can tell."

No, he's going to break my heart when he finishes whatever business he came for and

241

leaves again, Gen thought. *And I'm going to make a fool of myself this time. This time, knowing what the pain of losing him is like, I won't be able to smile bravely.*

But she couldn't say those words, and Lucy left the room. Genevieve was alone with Lucas.

"I didn't mean to disrupt your class," he said.

She made a pathetic attempt at a smile and shook her head. "It was almost over. I was almost ready to leave."

"Then I'm keeping you from something."

I would break any appointment for you, she thought. "No. Nothing."

"No . . . date? I've been told that you have a man harem that trails you around." He smiled slightly, but the smile was fleeting.

"They're . . . boys. I don't date them."

"Who do you date?" he asked. Then he swore. "Don't answer that. I was out of line asking."

"I don't date," she answered. "Who do *you* date?" She was afraid to know. She *needed* to know. Maybe hearing about his newest relationship would make it easier to stop loving him and she could get through this conversation without making a fool of herself.

"You," he said. "In my dreams."

Her heart began to pound; she couldn't catch her breath. Surely he was joking. Lucas had made it clear that he couldn't be a forever man. He never came back once he was gone. Whirling, trying to regain some composure, she tried to think of something light to say, something that wouldn't reveal how much he affected her. "Those must be nightmares of my first days here when I didn't know what I was doing." She aimed for light and teasing, but her throat closed up. Tears threatened. She started to gather up the containers of paint on the table, hoping that her busy hands would project a composure that her voice belied.

Then his hands were on her shoulders. "I shouldn't have said that. I know it's not what you'd want to hear." His touch . . . she leaned back slightly. It had been so long since she'd felt his touch, but . . . he was apologizing to her and —

"No," she said, turning so that she was facing him now and almost right up against him. She breathed in his scent and felt her heart helplessly going into a fast free fall. "Don't apologize to me. You were just teasing and I'm a strong woman. Right? You helped me learn to be strong."

"You were always strong. Deep inside. You'd simply buried it." His hands crept up to frame her face. "I admired you from the first and I . . . What if I wasn't teasing, Gen?"

A tiny glimmer of hope came to life deep in her heart, but she tried to sidestep it. If Lucas *was* dreaming of her, then he wouldn't see that as a good thing. Love had always been a hurtful thing in his world. If he had dreams of her . . . maybe he was here for one last look. Because reality often killed dreams.

She looked up into his eyes, afraid to hope, afraid of everything. She hated that. "Are they good or bad dreams?" she asked.

He closed his eyes and pulled her to him. "How can you ask that?"

"I . . . I don't know. I guess I asked because . . ." She faltered. *Because I love you but I can't tell you. Because I don't want to be one of those women you'll regret forever.*

"Maybe you asked because I'm such an idiot. Because I've kept the truth from you. I've always walled myself off. But, Gen . . . being with you . . . being *away* from you, I realize that a life walled off from everyone is no life at all. When you smiled, my world came alive. When you laughed with me, the world was a thousand times better just because you were there.

"I hid my heart to shield it, but . . . Gen,

you make me want to risk everything."

Genevieve's whole body felt like one big teardrop. She opened her mouth, hoping she could find her voice, but all that came out was one half-sobbed "Lucas."

He held up his hand. "You don't *have* to say anything if you don't want to. You don't ever have to love me. It's okay if you don't, but I love *you,* and I can never go back to living behind my walls again. You did that. You opened that door for me."

Tears threatened to drop from her lashes. She dashed them away and stood tall. She frowned. "So . . . it's okay if I don't love you."

He took a deep visible breath and something she couldn't quite decipher flashed in his eyes. He turned to the side and opened his mouth. In half a second flat, Genevieve placed her fingertips over his lips. "Don't lie," she whispered. "I love you so much it's killing me being apart from you. You don't have to lie."

He closed his eyes, he pulled her to him, so close she could barely breathe. "Good, because I love you so much that I can't even function. Staying away from you all this time has been torture."

"Worse than torture," she said.

"I didn't mean to come spoil things for

245

you. I know how important it is for you to be able to stand alone."

She pulled back slightly and looked into his eyes. "Yes, but being with you, loving you changed everything. You gave my life back to me, but I'd rather *share* my life. With you, I can still be independent and strong and . . . yours, too."

A smile like she'd never seen lit up Lucas's gorgeous face. He dropped a kiss on her lips, hard and fast, and then another slower, simmering one. "You are delicious, wonderful . . . and . . . I can't believe that you love me."

"I can't believe I can finally say it. I can shout it from the rooftops. I love Lucas McDowell, world!" She rose on her toes and kissed the side of his mouth.

"Does this mean that . . . Genevieve, will you marry me?"

"I'll marry you this minute. As long as you love me."

"I'll never give you reason to doubt it. In fact . . ." He dropped to one knee. "I'm afraid I don't have a ring. I came here, promising myself that I wouldn't try to tie you to me by spilling my heart."

Genevieve put her hands on her hips. "I would have hated it if you hadn't spilled your heart." Although, of course, she would never have known. "Lucas, Lucas, I'm so glad you told me."

"I couldn't seem to stop myself."

She tilted her head and gave him a sly look. "Mr. I-need-to-be-in-control."

He chuckled. "You seem to make me lose all that hard-earned control."

"Good." She placed her palms on his chest, reveling in the freedom to touch him at will. "And I don't need a ring. I've got everything I want in you."

He grinned. "You are amazing and special and more than I will ever deserve and I fully intend to get you a diamond that will weigh your hand down. You can put it in a box if you don't want it, but I need to give it to you. Still, for today . . . even though I don't have the ring, I do have something I think you'll like."

He pulled a small box out of his pocket. It was larger than a ring box and deeper. He flipped it open. Inside lay a very small, very delicate castle with a silver sheen to it. He held it out to Genevieve.

Genevieve recognized it immediately. "Lucas. Oh . . . where did you find this?" She took the castle, slipped her finger in a hole in the bottom and popped out a pretty silver thimble. "I haven't seen this in forever. I thought it was lost."

"I found it in a display of your parents' work in Austria. This was part of a group of glass thimbles they had made, but . . . one look at this and I was sure it was *your* work. Am I right?"

She nodded. "It was one of the few things I ever made. My father thought it was ridiculous."

"That may have been what he said, but he liked it enough that he and your mother included it in one of their shows. This shows that they really did appreciate you."

One tear that had threatened trickled down.

"Gen? I'm so sorry." He wiped the tear from her cheek with the pad of his thumb. She shivered from his touch and moved closer.

"Don't be sorry. I'm not sad."

"What are you, then, my love?"

"I'm strong, I'm independent, I'm a force to be reckoned with."

He raised one dark eyebrow. "You forgot one thing."

"I forgot two. I'm loved by the most wonderful man in the world and I'm in love with him. Now, can I ask you one thing, Lucas?"

"Ask away."

"When are you going to kiss me again."
He laughed. "Now. Very definitely now."

EPILOGUE

It had been three months since he and
Genevieve had married, they had been
traveling the world, continuing their work
and setting up the second Angie's House.
But today they had arrived back in Chicago,
where they'd bought a home, and Genevieve, his lovely, wonderful Genevieve was
in her element, in her studio, creating some
amazing pieces that would make a lucky art
collector very happy.

"Lucas, I have something I need to show
you," she said. He turned with a smile on
his face, fully expecting her to be holding
some fragile bit of glass. Instead, she held
out pieces of paper.

"They're drawings and letters from our
ladies in Chicago," she said. "And . . ."

Lucas frowned. Genevieve was not a
woman to falter or look uncomfortable, but
lifting her head, she gazed up at him with
uncertainty in her pretty green eyes. "This

one is special," she said, held out a solitary sheet of plain white paper with a photo attached. The photo was of a pretty woman and a child of about eleven. There was no scar visible on the woman's face, because she was presenting her other side, but he knew it was there just the same. Beneath the photo was a brief note:

Lucas, I know I told you I didn't want anything and that I refused to take anything more than you'd given us, but your wonderful wife is a very persuasive woman. Gen . . . found us. We're safe. We're finally happy and free. I forgave you a long time ago. Now I can finally forgive myself, too. Thank you for this place. Thank you always. Louisa

Lucas closed his eyes. He turned away, an emotional battle raging inside him.

"I know it was wrong to do this behind your back," Genevieve said softly. "You'd think a woman like me who prides herself on doing everything herself, would never cross that line. But you named the house for her and hurting her had hurt you. I didn't want your past to hurt you anymore and . . .

"Louisa told me that you had located her

before you'd ever met me. She was the first person you invited to Angie's House and she turned you down. Despite those dreams she'd had, she wanted and needed to break all ties to her past. I knew then, that I'd made a serious mistake. I'd breached your trust and I —"

Lucas whirled then. He pulled Genevieve into his arms, kissing her, raising her high on his body until his lips were against her throat. "I can't believe you did this for me, that you risked so much for me and . . . how did you get her to agree?"

He lowered Genevieve slowly until they were eye to eye, heart-to-heart. "I sent the best delegation I could think of, the women who have known the types of hardships Louisa has and who have grown to love you. I sent the women of Angie's House to Angie. They took her into their hearts — they persuaded Della to let them bring a child into their midst. In short, they loved Angie and her daughter until she just couldn't say no. And I — I'm sorry that I interfered in your private life, Lucas. But I'd do it again in a heartbeat. Love makes a woman do incredibly risky things."

"Thank goodness, my love. And . . . those women of yours . . ."

She shook her head, smiling at him. "No.

Those women are yours, too. You changed their worlds, Lucas."

"We did it together," he said. "You and I."

She smiled at him. "Lucas?"

He tilted his head and looked at her, waiting.

"*We* did something else," she said. "Something besides Angie's House." Then she reached out, took his hand and placed it on her abdomen. "We created a miracle."

Joy filled his soul. "I think I was given a miracle when you walked into my life."

"And I'm never walking out," she promised.

He kissed her lips. "I'll hold you to that promise."

She smiled against his mouth. "I'm counting on that." Then she kissed him again. The letter fell from her hand to the ground, but it didn't matter. He had his miracle and his love in his arms.

ABOUT THE AUTHOR

Myrna Mackenzie grew up not having a clue what she wanted to be (she hadn't been born a princess, the one job she thought she might like because of the steady flow of pretty dresses and crowns), but she knew that she loved stories and happy endings, so falling into life as a romance writer was pretty much inevitable. An award-winning author who has written more than thirty-five novels, Myrna was born in a small town in Dunklin County, Missouri, grew up just outside Chicago and now divides her time between two lakes in Chicago and Wisconsin, both very different and both very beautiful. She adores the internet (which still seems magical after all these years), loves coffee, hiking, attempting gardening (without much success), cooking and knitting. Readers (and other potential gardeners, cooks, knitters, writers, etc.) can visit Myrna online at www.myrnamackenzie

.com, or write to her at P.O. Box 225, La Grange, IL 60525, U.S.A.

The employees of Thorndike Press hope you have enjoyed this Large Print book. All our Thorndike, Wheeler, and Kennebec Large Print titles are designed for easy reading, and all our books are made to last. Other Thorndike Press Large Print books are available at your library, through selected bookstores, or directly from us.

For information about titles, please call:
(800) 223-1244

or visit our Web site at:
http://gale.cengage.com/thorndike

To share your comments, please write:
Publisher
Thorndike Press
10 Water St., Suite 310
Waterville, ME 04901